Shadows of the Blue Forest

Luc Rynolds

Contents

1

CHAPTER 1

A campfire burns in middle of the Blue forest, some horses tied to a post, few men eating and drinking around the fire, their faces turn brighter with every crackle in fire. Blue forest is trying its best to remain dark and stop the moonlight with its big trees, but moonlight make the forest a little bright by making its way through the leafs. Moon is shining bright as it's the night of the full moon,

Two eyes looks at moon angrily because moon was making his work difficult, then those eyes make their way to a face near the fire, once again eyes look up and sees the moon with a little anger. That face near the fire is known to be the nicest man in whole lands, his name is "Henry Charles" or "Lord Henry Charles", lord of the green plains, every man knows him and happy to meet him as he Is famous for his charming personality. The man stalking him in the shadows is known by many names, 'The unwanted'; 'Shadow Death' or the most famous 'Red shadow'.

Henry stood up and walked towards his tent, two of his guards followed him and stood beside his tent, Henry went in for a good night sleep. His men still sitting around fire and their laughs echoed in forest time to time. Shadow starts walking around the camp to the back of Henry's tent. He knows he only got little time because Henry's men will be getting up after their lord left, now they have to go to their posts to protect the camp from wild animals.

He make it to Henry's tent, he knew he would be sleep as he watched him drink for past two hours, He put his dagger through the tent's cloth and cuts it making a little hole, His eyes sees Henry on the bed, rhythm of his chest told Red that he is sleeping. He heard clanking of pots and swords meaning that Henry's men are ready for their duties, He quickly take out his blow darts and load the tube with a dart, dart was attached to a thread and dipped in a lethal poison. He put the tube through the hole and blew in it. Dart went flying in Henry's arm.

Henry did not move due to his drunken night. Shadow heard the guards coming and starts to pull the thread. As soon as he recovers the dart, He ran on his four to keep out of sight and into the woods, vanishing into the darkness of the great Blue Forest.

2

CHAPTER 2

Lord Dake Artis was walking to his castle with his loyal servant Renald. Lord Artis is a well-built man with brown hair and he is in his fifties. Renald was short twenty five years old. They were talking about the death of Lord Henry. Lord Artis' lands were beside Lord Henry's lands.

Lord Artis: What is the reaction of locals?

Renald: They think Red Shadow is behind this.

Lord Artis: and why is that?

Renald: No snake with the black fry poison is in Blue Forest plus his camp was heavily guarded, no simple assassin can get past the guards.

Lord Artis: no guard was killed? Or any guard saw anything?

Renald: Nope.

Lord Artis: Well send my respects to his locals, I will visit them myself in afternoon.

Renald bowed then turn around and walked out towards the fruit farms which belonged to Lord Artis.

Lord Artis stood watching him until he walked out. His face indicated that he is in deep thoughts. Then he walked in his castle, he passed his hallways. His ancestor's pictures were hung on the wall. He was going to his study but when he passed his bathrooms, he heard someone taking bath and singing.

He became angry as these were his personal baths and no servant was allowed to use them. He rushed into baths and yelled.

Lord Artis: Who the hell thinks they can use my baths....come out, I will skin you alive.

Lord Artis noticed that bathroom was dark, only one torch was lit and others were out. A voice came from behind the curtain.

"Relaaax, it's just some water."

Lord Artis recognized the voice and quickly locked the bath door.

Lord Artis: Oh it's you Red, I was wondering who in my servants became brave enough to use my bath.

Red: hahaha, I waited for you in your study but going through the forest made me tired, Bath always make me fresh.

Lord Artis asked anxiously: So?

Red: Yes, it does make me fresh.....

Lord Artis face showed a little anger and he said.

" Talking about your assignment "

Red: oh yeah, that is done.....was pretty easy.

Lord Artis: Locals are already saying it was you. You used Black fry to kill him.

Red starts to wear cloths behind curtain.

Red: I had to make a little announcement, I could kill him with any poison but it's kind of my mark. How would I receive any more assignments if no one knows that a big man like Lord Henry was killed in his own tent.

Lord Artis watched him as he came out from behind the curtain, he was wearing his black leather armor with a sword on the side. They both came out of the bathroom and starts to walk towards his study.

Lord Artis: Not going to lie...I tried some other paid killers but no one wanted to go after Henry and those who agreed, did not want to go in the Blue forest.

They entered the study and both sits on chair face to face.

Red: Who else agreed to kill him??

Lord Artis: That young boy "Rio", I heard his name a lot, locals fear him now.

Red: eh, just a new kid......well let's talk some gold, shall we?

Lord Artis smiled and opened his desk; he took out a medium sized sack.

Lord Artis: as requested.

Red took the sack and looked in while Lord Artis pour some wine in two glasses. Then he think about something and pour it back in the jug.

Red stood up, shook his hand and said.

Red: you can drink the wine, nothing in it.

Lord Artis: Na, cannot risk it, in fact I will open a new barrel

...

Red smiled and walked towards the back gate, no one can see him with Lord Artis or leaving his castle.

Lord left out a big breath of relief, his face showed happiness, he walked to the gate but stopped.

He turned around and came to the pad on which he leaves instructions for Renald, he picks up a pen from the ink pot and wrote on the pad

"Waste all barrels of wine, and stock new ones, immediately"

3

CHAPTER 3

Welcome to the beautiful and peaceful Land of Draound. Legend has it that very long ago there was no name for these grassy plains. These grassy plains cover thousands of acres, many valleys and 3 big forests make these grassy plains. From one side this place was cut off by a sea called "Crystal Sea".

And from one side it was covered by small and big mountain ranges with different names, from the third side it had Blue Forest which was very vast and seem to have no end to it. from the fourth side it was connected to the world by land called "Miller Passage", But as beautiful as it was, it was also a victim for the savages for looting. Stories tell that these savages often come from the other side of the mountains and attack the villages.

Stories also mention of all these magical creatures' savages brought with them like trolls and ogres, they use to eat humans and help savages in looting. Then a twenty one year old boy stood up, a farmer's son named Draound. Draound was the first voice against these savages and slowly many brave souls started to support him. Then Draound and his army fought against the enemy in a great battle and destroyed them once and for all, army chased them through the plains, up on the mountains until they were out of these lands.

It's also been said that Draound's first kill was a troll; he cut him in half with one swing of his sword. Draound beat the enemies and people named these lands after him. He was offered a throne, to be the king but he refused and remained a farmer. Land of Draound still has no king and different lords with their own armies own their parts and rule them. Still when travelers go up in mountains they tell the tales that still there are of signs of a great battle.

But legends are legends, now no one knows if these are true or just some stories mothers tell their children. Now there are many lords but there are four big lords in this land including Lord Henry and Lord Artis. There are 3 forests and biggest of them is Blue forest which spreads outside of Land of Draound, it goes with the Miller Passage. Blue forest is the most dangerous place in all the lands; it is filled with darkness as sunlight hardly reaches in through the thick forest.

It's been famous for myths and lost adventurers.....some bones were recovered with animal attack signs and others are still waiting to be discovered. Some say that still the troll and ogres are living in there, waiting in the dark, waiting to come out again, waiting to kill and eat. In these lands there is also one more name famous but it's famous for fear and death.

"Red Shadow" the name of fear for locals, everybody knows his name but only some have seen him and fewer of those are alive but not to tell tales. Nobody knows Red's real name, they only know that he is a paid killer and is the top name of his profession and now rumor has it that Lord Henry was killed by Red Shadow. Red's fear is on the rise once again.

4

CHAPTER 4

Rio was sitting in the local pub, he was a young boy with a talent for killing, he was new in this work but already making quite a name and also few companions. Rio had a scar on his right cheek which he received in a fight, his hair were brown and had bright eyes. He thought of Red as his biggest rival but Red never paid any attention. Now he sits in pub with his gang talking about Lord Henry.

Rio: That job came to me first but I declined.

His man looked at him, and he continued to speak.

"Only idiots will go in the Blue forest, and Henry was one of them. People don't go there in broad day and that fool went camping there in night".

Some soldiers on a nearest table heard him; one of them turns to him and said:

"Watch your mouth boy, Lord Henry was many things but not a fool".

These were Henry's soldiers and like all locals loved him because of his niceness.

Rio smiled at him and said.

Rio: He was indeed many things, but also a fool, what did he thought that just because he is nice to you idiots, you can protect him in the Blue forest? If that's the case, he is dead for good"

Soldier's face turned red with anger and he stood up with his hand on the sword and said.

"You are just some words away from getting your tongue cut in hundreds of pieces"

Before Rio could reply a kid ran in and said to the soldier.

"Trouble at inn, you are needed there quickly"

Soldier looks at Rio and said.

"Your luck just saved you boy", then he goes out followed by his comrades.

Rio loses his grip on his knife under the table. He Smiled at his friends and said.

Rio: That was a close one.

While soldiers were following the child who led them to the nearest inn where a crowd was starting to gather. They made their way to the center of the crowd where two men were lying. One man's head was crushed and his both legs were cut, or so as it seemed. Second man's eyes were closed and looked like he was taking his last breaths. He was saying and repeating some words I very low voice.

"Mountain.....run".

"Get some water' someone shouted.

But His body took some shakes and then he stopped breathing.

Crowd started whispering as soldiers began to investigate the witnesses.

Past five days were very strange for people. First Lord Henry died and on the next day two travelers died in a weird manner, afterwards three miners went missing near the mountains. A whole family of eight people vanished near Blue forest and on the next day it happened again with five soldiers. With No Lord in Henry's place, nobody was to look into this matter. Lord Henry lived alone with no heir. Closest Lord was Lord Artis who put his son in charge of his land and took over lord Henry's place. In normal circumstances it would not be so easy, other lords would go against Dake but right now immediate attention was required to missing and killings.

Right now the group of same soldiers was reporting to Lord Artis in Lord Henry's castle.

Captain of these soldiers was Jonald Kane who was explaining everything to Lord Artis.

Jonald: Witnesses saw him running scared with other body on his shoulders. He was running and yelling gibber gabber. After reaching the inn he just fell and spoke some nonsense.

Lord Artis: and what was this nonsense?

Jonald: just two words my lord; he spoke them over and over again.

Lord Artis: speak them for me.

Jonald: Mountain...run.

Jonald's voice echoed in the throne room.

Lord Artis: Pretty clear. Miners went missing near the mountains too... check those mountain for anything...form a search party.

Lord Artis's order turned soldiers faces a little worried. Jonald looked at them and said.

Jonald: My lord, that may not be possible, soldiers are scared.

Lord Artis laughed and said.

"What kind of men are you?"

Jonald felt insulted.

"My lord, head of that man was not smashed by any weapon"

"By a rock?"

"No my lord, seemed it was pressurized by something... also limbs were not cut but pulled till they were torn apart"

"And that scares you?"

"Any man would be scared my lord"

"You will take your men on the mountains"

"What if they die my lord?"

"I don't care captain"

Jonald looked at Lord Artis in surprise and anger; then he said. Jonald: My lord, I cannot lead my man in to the unknown danger.

Lord Artis shouted: What a bunch of little girls, I order you to do so.

Anger spread on Jonald's face, he turned to his soldiers and with a little nod, ordered them to go outside. Soldiers start walking towards the door. Then Jonald said to Lord Artis.

Jonald: I don't take orders from you.....my lord. You are not lord of grassy plains by law.

Then he turned around and started walking. Lord Artis turned red with anger but he tried to keep himself calm, he said.

Lord Artis: I am just trying to look after the innocent people of your beloved Lord Henry, and right now only Grassy Plains is getting affected, I don't need you but your people need you.

Jonald didn't stop, he keeps on walking and said.

"We are keeping the peace in grassy plains already, but if you think I am going to take my man in unknown danger, then think again my lord.

Lord Artis watched him leave, He stood up from throne and started walking towards the halls leading to inner parts of castle, he wanted to rest.

5

CHAPTER 5

Land of Draound was hearing rumors; all Lords were trying their best to keep their people calm.

In grassy plains patrols were set and no one was allowed to go towards the mountains or the Blue Forest. In past week, two miners were found dead, some parts of body missing and at the same time some kids who went missing near Blue forest and nobody were brave enough to go in.

Stories went flying to other valleys and people started getting scared. Lord Artis was receiving letters from other lords in which he was asked to control the situation. Lord Artis was uncertain of what to do and what not. His army was in his valley and right now he was kind of a usurper on grassy plains and could not risk calling his army here because any other lord can see this as an opportunity and attack his valley.

As for Henry's army, they were busy with Henry's people. They were doing a good job so Lord Artis was happy that its one less of headache for him. But this new situation made him worried. Lord Artis walked into the throne room where he had called army commanders. He walks up to the throne, sits on it and look to their faces.

In front of him was standing general Salvador and general Riendo.

Lord Artis: Where is the captain I summoned for?

Salvador: He refuses to come my lord.

Lord Artis: He is doing a good job in the streets so I will overlook his foolishness.

Riendo: my lord, he is a good kid but he is just......

Lord Artis did not let him finish and said in anger.

"Did I ask you to be his mother general?"

"No my lord .....forgive me"

"Hm.....what is the report from the mountains?"

"My lord, Our soldiers refuse to go. They think some un-natural things are at work there, I took two men with me and investigated but found nothing."

"So miners are turning into thin air? That's what you are saying?"

"N..NO my lord, it snowed fresh there so no prints could be spotted"

"Anything unusual?"

"No my lord, we stayed the night too but nothing happened, I have left them both up and instructed them to report as soon as they notice anything unusual"

Lord Bake put his head down and thinks...then he looks to General Salvador.

"You command our mounted battalion Salvador, what is the status report of patrols?"

"My lord, patrols are ongoing as planned, both horses and men are on duty day and night. Blue forest cannot be accessed from grassy plains. Nothing unusual has been reported"

Lord Artis sighs and says.

Lord Artis: We have a situation on our hands gentlemen, what do you think? Who is behind this?

Salvador: Bandits?

Lord Artis: They don't and cannot tear people's body parts off. I think a wild animal is on the mountain.

Riendo: But my lord, what about the blue forest?

Salvador: No one want to go in there, can you Riendo?

Riendo: I can if my lord commands.

Lord Artis: Someone needs to do it, get ready.

Lord Artis put his head down again....both generals look at him.

Lord Artis cracked his fingers and look at them both and says:

Lord Artis: Well generals both of you can go, you are doing good job, keep me informed if we make any progress.

Both generals bowed and went out of the throne room while Lord Artis took sips of wine. He fills up his glass again and looks at wine, his face show that he remembered something ... after a while he starts again to take sips.

Lord Artis was walking to his bedroom, he was very tired because he took a tour of the valley to inspect the condition of patrols till noon and rest of the day he had to sit in throne room to solve problems of people like miners were stopped to go to mountains so now they were out of jobs and now throne has to pay them.

He walks in his bedroom and sits on bed. He removes his shoes, then his socks, and then he removes his shirt.

A voice echoed in the room.

"I would leave the pants on if I were you".

Lord Artis: Don't worry, I knew you were here, noticed that all torches were out.

Red comes out from a dark corner of the room, he had his sword on the side and his black armor on.

"Why did you call me?"

"I need help"

"I do not help people"

"I know, I know, I will pay"

"Task?"

"Have to investigate something"

"I don't investigate things"

"You have to, only this time"

"I kill only, ask someone else"

"No one would do it"

"And Why? If I may know"

Lord Artis looks at him for a while.

"No one would go in the Blue Forest"

Red laughed, his voice filled the room.

"Why would I go in there? Do you not know, ogres live there"

Lord Artis smiled a little at his joke.

"You know strange events going on"

"Everybody knows"

"Have to solve this matter"

"Then do it, why need me?"

"No one want to go in there except for a general but i do not think he will come out alive and i need him here because he obeys me and believe me i am not in the position to lose obedient people right now, I know you can go because you killed Henry there and came out alive too"

"I never went in Blue Forest before that, I only went in because that fool Henry went in and I follow my target even in hell"

"That's why you have to help me"

"I don't investigate, when you need a dead man then you can call me"

"I gave you a job to kill Henry so I can take over his lands, we were the most powerful lords in whole land of Draound, now I am the only one, thanks to you but if I don't solve this matter everyone will go against me, lords and locals will overthrow me"

"Ask someone else"

Lord Artis crackles his fingers.

"No one will do it, even Rio was afraid to go in the forest, do this job and I will give you a valley in the grassy plains, also no one from the law will touch you, you will not get a chance like this"

Red muscles got tense and he thought for a second

"I think i can make an exception"

Lord Artis sighs in relief and smiled. "When will you go, I will pull back patrols from there"?

"No need, I have been stealing there food for two days, they won't stop me"

Red walked up to the door and opens it but Lord Artis's voice stops his feet.

Lord Artis: Do you know Jonald, a young captain.

Red tried to remember and says.

Red: yeah, good lad, he is been controlling the valley pretty good. Once he almost made me lose my target.

Lord Artis: Kill him. After all this mess is over.

A bloody smile danced on Red's face.

"With pleasure"

As Red walks out, Lord Artis shouts.

Lord Artis: You forgot to tell me the price.

Red's voice echoes in the dark hallway like cold wind

"This one is on the House"

Lord Artis felt a chill in his body.

The night was silent, Jonald and his man were on patrol, Jonald was working very hard nowadays because he was born in grassy plains, this was his home and he loved his home. These killings were affecting grassy plains and it was very sad for him. Jonald was very popular among locals. He helped everybody in need. Tonight he was patrolling near the Blue Forest. Many times he thought of going in the forest to see what was happening but could not go. Suddenly Jonald's party saw some soldiers running toward them, Jonald quickly ran towards them. When they reach each other Jonald asked them.

Jonald: What happened?

Soldier: We saw someone, threw a Knife at us and ran in this direction.

Jonald: No one came here, search the area and get back to your post.

Soldier looked confused but they obeyed the order and went back.

Jonald became very confused, all of a sudden he felt like someone is watching him. He looked towards the forest but there was nothing but darkness and animal's voices. He shook his head and started walking but little did he know that two bloody eyes were watching him from the forest.

6

CHAPTER 6

Two shadows were moving fast in the darkness of the Blue Forest, they both were running. These two were soldiers sent by Jonald. After Lord Artis ordered General Riendo not to go in Blue Forest to investigate, Jonald wanted to go in there himself but his men asked him to stay as he was needed in the valley.

These two soldiers volunteered to go in on a very strict command from Jonald that they will come back before nightfall. But these unlucky souls lost their way in the thickness of the forest and now were running scared. They tried their best to find the way but couldn't and now it was night and moonlight were unable to reach in the forest.

Suddenly they started hearing growling behind them, seemed like a wild animal got their scent. They started running fast and trying to find their way through trees, all of a sudden they stumbled upon an open area with no trees. Moonlight was making the view clear and they could see the Blue bushes covering the ground. These bushes covered all the ground in this forest that is why it was called Blue Forest. They both heard the growling again and one of them shouted

"Come on, in the middle, we have a better chance"

Both ran in the middle of that open area and took their swords out. Swords made a loud sound and they heard the growling again, both stood back to back with swords in their hands. Suddenly one said

"Over there"

From that direction, a beast came into the moonlight. Its skin was pale and its size was of a horse, it had sharp teeth and face looked like a wolf, it was taking slow steps towards them, growling goes louder with every step and his fangs started to shine in moonlight.

It took a stop and started running towards them. Both soldiers got ready to fight. Beast came close and jumped on them. They both slides to their sides, beast went past them from the middle and quickly turn around. Both soldiers got forward to attack, one of them swung his sword which hit the beast on its back. His swing was with full strength but swords could only cut through beast's skin and two inches further. Beast growls painfully and jumped over them taking his sword from his hand stuck in its hard flesh.

Second soldier turned. Beast reached him quickly to attack. He swung his sword but before he could hit the beast, beast chewed his face. Blood started gushing which turned the beast more aggressive. Beast started chewing his face. Other soldier saw this in horror and reached for his sword which fell to the ground during beast's attack. First soldier fell to the ground. Beast started biting his neck to finish him off.

Other soldier looked at them; he was never been this much scared in his whole life. He thought of attacking but he saw what happened to his first attack, he could not finish this beast alone. He saw that beast was busy with the body; Soldier saw this as an opportunity and started running towards the trees. Beast did not pay any attention as it tasted human flesh for the first time. As soon as he entered the trees, a shadow grabbed him by the arm and started running to the left side. Soldier followed him mindlessly.

Soldier's ear were listening to sounds of birds, he opened his eyes and saw blue sky, golden sunlight was touching his face, he felt so relaxed, he kept listening to the chirping of birds and feeling the warmth of sun on his face but suddenly he remembered last night. He quickly sits up and looked around. He saw trees around him. He was on a wooden platform on a tree. Different stuff was all around him, some baskets of different fruits, pots and other daily use stuff, most of which was made of wood. His sword and dagger were lying in a corner.

He started remembering last night. After the shadow grabbed him, they both ran for some time, they went through a stream and then climbed this tree. He was so scared that he did everything the shadow did without saying anything.

After that shadow left, leaving him alone here. Soldier did not remember when he slept.

He only remember that he was wearing his dagger and sword, now they are lying in the corner meaning that whoever that shadow returned after. Soldier stood up and grabbed his sword. He took a look on the forest which seemed so beautiful, he could see colorful birds on trees, and then he looked down and saw blue ground. He said to himself.

"Damn these blue Bushes, damn everything which is blue".

He started climbing down the tree, small holes were made into the tree to climb, he reached ground and looked up, It was almost thirty feet climb. He heard stream sound and he took out his sword and started walking. Animal voices were echoing in the forest. He saw someone sitting at the stream. He started walking fast. He reached the stranger who was filling his canteen. He stood behind him and said.

Soldier: Who are you?

Stranger slowly stood up.....Soldier pointed his sword towards him. Stranger started drinking his water.

Soldiers shouted again.

"I said who are you, answer me or I will have your head"

Stranger spoke for the first time.

"What is your name soldier?"

It was a voice of a women, soldier did not heard any sweeter voice then this voice in his whole life.

Soldier said again. "I asked you, who are you?"

Woman sat again and started filling her canteen. Her sweet voice answered soldier.

"I rescued you last night, don't be afraid....What is your name?"

Soldier thought for a moment then replied.

"Max".

"Max, max......what a beautiful name. Very fitting for a soldier"

Woman stood up and turned around. Max felt like he was seeing a dream. In front of max stood an Elf.

Max only heard myths about Blue Forest and ogres but never heard of an elf, she was wearing deer skin cloths and wore little dagger on the side, Max was getting scared again, he was going out of breath and his sword started shaking. He sat on the ground and held his head with his both hands. Elf looked at him and said.

"Relax, breath and don't be scared"

Max asked her in shaky voice.

"What are you?'

Elf smiled at him, she came near him and picked up his sword.

"I am an Elf, and by looking at you I can say that you have never seen one, also you are still under effect of last night".

Max looked at her, she gave him his sword and helped him up. They both started walking towards the tree. Max looked at her and said.

"Thank you for saving me".

She smiles and said.

"don't thank me yet, you are not safe until you get out this forest, last night I saw you both running blindly and saw that beast behind you, Sorry about your friend".

They started climbing the tree. Max followed her to the platform.

"Who are you?" max asked.

She looked at him and throws an apple at him.

"Its best that you don't know, Eat up, you have to leave"

Max didn't want to upset her as she was a mythical creature. He ate some apples while she explained him the way out, it was a day walking. Max understood that last day they were going in the opposite direction of the grassy plains, they were too deep in the forest. After that max wore his sword and dagger, he thanked her again and climbed down the tree. He walked to the stream and looked behind to her, she waved to him and he crossed the stream then went out of her sight. She sat back and looked up to the sky. It was a nice morning, she laid back, closed her eyes. She fell asleep.

After some time, she felt something touching her arm; she opened her eyes and saw Max poking her with a stick.

"What are you doing here" she asked angrily.

"I lost the way a little after I entered the trees across the stream."

She slapped away the stick.

"It's not safe for you here" she stood up and started wearing her sword.

After that she looked to Max and said

"I can take you to the forest's end, but no one must see me".

Max nodded and they started climbing down the tree. Then they crossed the stream and started walking. Max could have never even imagined that Blue Forest was so beautiful. Elf instructed max to not to make any noise and always lay low. They walked and walked, at noon they took some rest and then started walking again. They encountered some Wild animals like gorillas and forest Dogs but they stayed low and managed to keep out of sight. Max tried to talk to her several times but she did not replied so max started focusing on the way. After all day walk at dusk they were some miles away from the Forest's end. Darkness was filling the forest quickly, they both looked shadows to each other. Elf was saying to Max

Elf: you cannot tell anyone about me.

Max: Relax, no one will ever know about you. But how will you go back?

Elf: I live here, I can travel in darkness. I have spent my whole life here.

Elf stopped and drank some water from her canteen. She turned around and gave it to Max.

Max raised his hand to take the canteen, before his hand could reach her hand , a sword came out of his chest, covered with his blood. Elf looks at him in shock, Max looks down to sword with pain and shock on his face, coughed some blood out and someone draws out the sword from his back. Elf saw another shadow standing behind falling Max's body and she quickly reached for her sword but before she could draw her sword, a powerful punch knocked her out.

7

—— · ——

CHAPTER 7

Lord Artis was sitting in his study; General Riendo, General Salvador and Jonald were sitting across his study table. Lord Artis placed a letter in front of them and sat back rubbing his forehead. They read the letter one by one and looked at Lord Artis. Lord Artis looked back at them. Silence was In the study room and then Jonald spoke.

Jonald: My lord, now?

Lord Artis: Now what? I cannot stop lord Philip to come to grassy plains.

Lord Salvador: My lord, I don't see the problem.

Lord Artis looks at him and laughed.

Lord Artis: Lord Philip is coming here to disrespect me; he is no lord but a mindless fighter. He is coming here so he can bring his fighters and as he say Help us with our problem, you know what he will do when he returns to his land? He will tell all people that Lord Artis could not handle his problems so he asked out Lord Philip's help. I don't want that disrespect Salvador.

Lord Salvador opened his mouth to say something but then he closes his mouth.

Lord Artis looks at Riendo and said.

"Any word from your lookouts?'

"No my lord, they have gone silent. They were suppose to come down for supplies last night"

"Well consider them dead, no one must know"

"Yes my lord, I already instructed my soldiers but to be sure I am going up myself tomorrow".

Lord Artis looked at Jonald, he asked him

"What is your report?"

"Valley is good my lord, everything is in order"

"You know Jonald, I admire you very much"

"My lord"

Then Lord Artis stood up, Three Army officials stood up too.

Lord Artis signed a paper and put the pen back in ink pot.

Lord Artis: Well gentlemen, you all are doing a good job, keep this up and we will wrap this up, now if you will excuse me I have to make arrangements for a mindless warrior's visit.

All three men stood up then bowed to Lord Artis and walked out. Lord Artis walked out in the hall way. A servant was dusting the Knight's armor decorated in the hallway. Lord Artis said to him.

"Go find Renald , tell him that I wish to see him in the garden and fetch me some wine".

Servant bowed and left. Lord Artis started walking towards outside. He wanted to get some fresh air. He was thinking about Red. Red left two days ago and has not returned. Lord Artis pulled back Riendo because Red was going in for investigation. He was getting a little worried about him, He was a skilled warrior without any doubt but he sent Red to the Blue Forest. He walked into the Garden which was in the courtyard of the castle. He saw Renald coming with a servant holding Wine jug and glasses.

Lord Artis sat on a bench, Renald reached him bowed. Lord Artis said.

"Sit"

Renald sat. Lord Artis Poured two glasses of wine and sent the servant away, he gave one to Renald and said.

"you know who is coming?"

"Lord Philip"

"Make arrangements, that idiot talks".

"Was busy making arrangements my lord, he will be comfortable".

"Any news of home?"

"Everything is good there".

Lord Artis took a sip and sat back, looking at the sky.

Her elf eyes opened slowly, She saw trees, she could see daylight. She tried to move but she was tied with her hands behind her back. She looked around, she was lying in a small cove, she saw her sword and dagger lying on the side, she looked once again but no one was there.

She quickly started crawling towards her weapons, she turned and grabbed the dagger with her tied hands and started cutting her ropes which were made from thick woody vines. She got free and quickly drew her sword. She came out very cautiously. She came out of the cove and look around, step by step walking slowly. Forest was echoing with birds chirping. She guessed that sun came up about two or three hours ago. She noticed someone lying between trees. She walked up to the body and saw someone lying face down, blood was all around the body but it was dry.

She could tell that whoever killed this person killed him during last night. She noticed that this person was wearing black leather armor so that meant it was not Max. She looked around again for Max body but did not saw any sign or blood or the body. She could not stay here to search more so she wore her sword again and started walking towards her home. She felt a little sore on her left side of the face.

She got punched pretty hard last night. She travelled on the same path she travelled last day with Max. Remembering Max made her a little sad, it was not that she had a soft heart but after all she saw a person after many years and talked with a human, this was first time in her life.

She did not stop to rest. When she saw any clear area, she started running and when heard any beast or wild animal she laid low. At afternoon she reached the stream, thanks to her running and also the fact that she was alone, she made it home in less time. A smile spread on her face when she saw her tree. She stepped into the stream, and started walking; she stopped in the middle and started splashing water on her face.

She cleaned her face properly and washed her hands then she drank some water. Her canteen was left back because she did not thought of finding it. She crossed the stream and slowly walked to her tree, climbed her way to the wooden platform. She was so tired that she did not even take off her weapons. She just went to her bed which she made from skins of different animals. She fell on it and went into deep sleep.

At mid night she felt very thirsty, her throat was dried up and she felt like needles in her throat. She wanted to ignore but thirst was too strong. She sat up and saw nothing but dark. She walked to her canteens piled up in the corner, opened one and drank the water. She turned towards the forest and closed her eyes. She felt soft wind touching her face, she felt so relaxed, she focused on the coldness of the environment. She felt chilled, she smiled a little with her eyes closed. She felt a much fainted whip of wind near her ear but before she could understand anything, a hand grabbed her face. She got shocked and resisted but something Was struck on her head and she felt falling into the darkness.

All sounds of forest started to faint and she completely blacked out.

At the same time, in the grassy plains a caravan entered. This was Lord Phillip and his companions. Lord Philip was a 52 year old man with one eye. His one eye was wasted during a conflict in his local tavern. This was when he was 30 year old and not a lord at that time. He killed seven people single highhandedly but lost an eye. Lord Philip was a great warrior and preferred to live like a soldier. In his company there were all very skilled soldiers and he live with them like any other soldier. He was coming to grassy plains because he hated Lord Artis, he always thought he was too mellow and never was worthy of being a powerful lord, this was his perfect chance to prove that. Lord Philip saw that sun has set so he ordered his comrades to make camp. One of his companions said.

"If we keep on moving then we can make it to the castle by mid night".

Lord Philip looked at him and smiled.

Lord Philip: What to do you want Dake to think? that we wanted to see his ugly face so badly that we marched to him as soon as we entered grassy plains. Make camp, enjoy this night and let Ludik deal with the cooking.

Ludik was one of his true friends. His loyal soldier and was one of the most skilled warrior in whole lands. Lord Philip made camp there, till midnight their laughing echoed in the silent valley of grassy plains. At the next morning, they found out that their three horses and two guards were disappeared leaving no sign but some blood stains.

8

CHAPTER 8

Once again she heard the sounds of the forest, but this time her head was hurting so bad that tears gather in her closed eyes. She opened her eyes and saw herself on her tree then she heard a cold voice.

"You know, when I was a kid.....my mother use to tell me bed time stories".

Elf turned herself in the voice's direction. She saw Red lying in her bed. Red Kept talking.

"She told me the stories of all the great warriors, all the heroes who fought great battles"

Elf noticed that Red was wearing the same armor as one which she saw on the dead body. Red kept speaking.

"She told me about the fallen ones, the victorious ones, about their weapons and about their companions".

"Who are you?" Elf asked him.

"But sometimes she told the stories which seemed like fairy-tales"

Elf shouted this time.

"Who are you?"

Red kept his eyes on her face and kept speaking.

"These stories had many inhuman entities in them, fighting beside great warriors".

Elf had a confused reaction but she said to Red again.

"Are you not listening? answer me, why have you captured me?"

"Ogres, trolls, fairies, giants, but you know who my favorite one was?"

Red was speaking; his face showed no expressions. Elf sat up.

"Elves, Elves were my favorite creatures." Red answered his own question.

"I always asked my mother, How can I meet them mother, but my mother always smiled at me and said that when you grow up then you will know how to. I grew up and I realized that those were just stories to help me sleep, until yesterday."

She looked at his face; he looked directly in her eyes and said.

"when sun came up yesterday, I could not believe myself. An elf was lying in front of me. I had to pinch myself to believe it." Then he laughed.

Elf looked at him and said.

Elf: Who are you?

Red: Call me by any name, does not affect me.

Elf: Why have you captured me?

Red: Someone will want to meet you.

Elf: Who?

Red: Someone.

She understood that he will not give him any information. She said.

Elf: I saw one of you dead this morning.

Red: It was me.

Elf: How are you alive?

Red (Smiled): I know some spells, can come back to life.

Elf did not know that whether he was joking or serious.

Elf: Did you let me go on purpose yesterday?

Red: Yes.

She understood that it was some kind of trick to make her think that he was dead. Then she remembered that max was killed there and she couldn't saw his body at the morning, He was just lying on Max's blood.

Elf: You followed me to see my home.

Red: Yes, if you call this tree your home.

Elf: Why?

Red: To know if there were more of you. but I have swept all surrounding area, you are all alone here.

Elf: What now?

Red: Some beasts are across the stream, wanted to have a midnight snack when I was looking for your kin. Until they leave, I am your guest.

Elf saw that his armor and cloths had dirt on them, and scratches were showing that meant he was in the forest more than one day. She thought that her enemy is too calm and seemed skilled so she had to be intelligent about it. She took a look on Red. Red had a hard featured face, he had broad shoulders. His armor was skin tight which showed that he have a built body with big arms. He had a sword by his side and one tube which she never saw before. Beside Red her fruit's basket was sitting, and he was eating apples. She was hungry but before she could say anything to him, Red understood her eyes and threw an apple at her.

"Eat up, keep up your strength, we have to walk all the way back".

She began to slowly eat, she was taking small bites. Red was looking at her and thinking that is she real or Red is having a dream. She looked up and Red threw another apple to her. Then again thought that she was his prisoner, not even tiny feelings must mix up with his work.

After sometime, Red tied her hands behind her back and put her on his shoulder and climbed down the tree then they cautiously walked to the stream and saw that beasts were gone. They started walking

Lord Artis was laughing and Lord Philip was sitting in front of him. They were sitting in study and Philip just told Dake about this morning. Lord Artis had tears in his eyes and he said.

Lord Artis: So you are saying that someone robbed The great warrior Philip, and took his two men from right under his nose?

Lord Philip: All right all right, I cannot guard my guards who are appointed to guard me.

Lord Artis: Well welcome to grassy plains, you just experienced the same problem, I am having. You are welcome to give any suggestion.

Lord Philip: Whoever they are, they have messed with me now. I got a report that you have pulled back your general from investigating Blue Forest.

Lord Artis took a sip of wine.

"Too dangerous, this army is not mine and I cannot lose a General who I trust."

"Then send some men"

"Forest will kill anyone, too dangerous"

"Oh come on, now you just exaggerating."

"Well you are welcome to waste your men"

Lord Philip smiled and said.

"I already sent some of my men to the Forest; They must be in the forest by now"

Lord Artis smiled and said

"Well consider them dead"

"They are ready to sacrifice themselves for their Lord"

"I have made arrangements for you and your men to stay, I would arrange a guest room for you but you won't use it, right?"

Lord Philip smiled at him. And said

"Any information about who is doing this?"

"NO, sent two men up on mountains, didn't return"

"any idea?"

"Nope, no one ever goes in mountains, it is like a maze and beyond mountain there are only wastelands or some travelers say."

"So we are sitting between two killer lands"

"You don't say"

They began to speak on other matters.

In the Forest, Philip's men were moving forward; they were only two miles in but were attacked by forest dogs one time. These were ten soldiers and their captain was a young fellow. They were moving cautiously. They were walking silently and were trying to find anything strange. Their boots were crushing blue bushes. With every voice they looked here and there in forest.

Captain: Be careful men.

Soldier: And we thought this was going to be just a little investigation.

Second Soldier: You were a fool to think that, don't you know there are mythical things in this forest like ogres and trolls.

All soldiers looked at him and laughed out loud.

Captain: Did your mother tell you that story last night? Grow up

All soldiers laughed again.

Captain while smiling said:

"hey, hey, sshhhh or ogres will hear you"

They all stopped laughing but kept smiling. They walked till noon but nothing happened. They did not see anything which can be reported. At noon they decided to walk back. They started to walk back so they can get out before forest turned dark.

As they walked for ten minutes, they came to a pond. This was not here when they came here.

Captain turned to his soldiers and said.

"Well congratulations boys, we have just lost our way"

Soldiers looked at each other, one said.

"we have to go back and start again"

Another soldier said.

"yeah, we are not far from where we stopped, but we have to be quick or ogres will eat us tonight"

Everybody looked at that soldier who told them the ogre story and laughed.

Suddenly one soldier said.

"shhh, someone is coming"

They all hid behind rocks and trees. They saw two persons coming, one was woman and other one was a man. Woman was tied with hands behind her back and man was holding her rope. They were all alone.

Captain gave the signal and they all came out, running towards them both. Woman got shocked and took a few steps back, while man was standing calm and did not do anything.

Soldiers surrounded them with swords in their hands. Captain walked up to them and said.

"Who are you?"

Man looked at him and said.

"I can ask you the same thing Soldier"

"Who are you?"

"Lord Philip knows me"

Captain smiled, and said.

"Anyone can recognize our uniforms, why you in Blue Forest and who is your prisoner"

Captain suddenly noticed woman's ears, he could not believe his eyes, he yelled

"It's an elf, it's an elf"

Soldiers looked at her too and their faces showed fear.

"Kill it, Kill it before it put a spell on us"

Another soldier said

"She is not a wizard you idiot"

They all were pointing their swords at them and were afraid.

A soldier yelled

"Captain, This is shadow death, I heard about him and his armor"

Captain looked at him. He noticed the armor and looked at the dart gun too.

"Arrest them both, Lord Philip will be happy"

Two soldiers grabbed the Elf, and two moved to Red, Red was standing silently, He let go of the rope and as soon soldiers got close, he took out his dagger and swung it while unsheathing it, One soldier's throat got cut opened and other one's got scared on his face. They both yelled and fell on the ground. Other soldiers quickly ran towards Red but Red was already running towards the trees. Two soldiers got in the trees behind him but captain called them back.

Captain: Come back, too dangerous in there, he won't survive alone.

Soldiers stopped and comeback. Now they all were staring at the Elf. She looked scared. Captain came near her and said.

"You know the way to the grassy plains?"

"No"

"Where the humans live"

"No"

Captain swung his hand, and a hard slap turned her face red.

"I don't like liars, if you co-operate I will not kill you"

Elf looked at him and said.

"you will take me to a lord too?"

"Yes"

"He will kill me"

"We will take you as our guest. You will be treated respectfully"

Elf did not believe him, but she could not do anything so she said.

"I do not know the way, I live in very deep, I have never come this way."

Captain lifts his hand to slap her but they all heard a loud growl. He looked at his soldiers and said.

"Hope Shadow death just met his death, let's move"

They started walking in the direction in which Red was taking her.

They walked till dusk but could not see anything familiar to the way of morning.

Captain interrogated the elf several time. But every time she said she came here for first time and Every time captain's hand left her face red, she turned more stone cold.

Soldiers found a cove, and captain told them that they will spend the night here.

Soldiers secured a perimeter around cove. They putted the elf in the cove and decided that they will take turns on the night watch.

9

CHAPTER 9

Soldiers woke up in the morning; they saw that one of them had disappeared in the night. He was on his guard duty. Upon sweeping the area, they found his bloody remains.

Soldier who told the ogre story said.

Soldier: Ogre got him man, I told you they are real.

Another soldier said.

"How do you know? They are not real you fool"

"We have an elf as prisoner, you still think they are not real?"

All soldiers went silent, this could be right.

Elf saw them all and said.

Elf: It was a beast.

Captain asked: Which beast?

Elf: Whose growl you heard near the pond.

Captain: How do you know?

Elf: four days ago, two men came in the forest and got attacked by this beast. Beast tasted human flesh now it wants this new taste again.

Captain: It could be forest dogs.

Elf: Only that beast is big enough to silently take a man away.

Captain started thinking. Soldiers started finding eatable things for breakfast. Captain ordered one soldier to climb a high tree and look for any sign which could tell in which direction they are going.

Soldier climbed the tree and after returning he said that he could see the mountains to the right side.

Mountains mean grassy plains. Captain got relaxed because at least he knew now in which direction they had to move. Soldiers gathered much kind of fruits; they untied the elf so she could eat too. They all started eating. After eating they went through their morning routines. Elf was given a little privacy between two rocks but rock was surrounded. After that they tied her up and started walking to their right side. Soldier told captain that it looked like two days journey. They kept walking.

In grassy plains, Lord Philip was informed that his soldiers have not returned yet. He was mocked by Lord Artis and was very angry. He ordered Ludik to form a party and go up to the mountains. Lord Artis advised him to not to send his man but Philip did not listened and ordered Ludik to go. Lord Artis ordered Jonald to go with them. Jonald and Ludik formed a party of eight men including them.

They wanted to move fast and move silently. Ludik wanted someone who knew the mountain. He believed that navigation plays a big part in a mission. Jonald tried to find someone but no one went up to the mountains. Jonald asked his soldiers to find Rio. He knew that one time Rio followed a thief up there. Now they were waiting for soldiers to return.

Ludik: Tell me, why a paid killer would catch a thief?

Jonald: A thief stole Lord Henry's crown, he once came into the market and when he got off his horse, his crown fell off and a thief picked it up and started running. Soldiers could not get him and they lost him in the crowd of market.

Ludik: So Henry put a handsome reward?

Jonald: Yup, we swept the valley, could not find him. Two days later, Rio showed up with the crown. We asked him where he found it, he told us that he tracked down the thief but before he could get him he rode away. Whole valley was looking for him so he rode to the mountains. Rio was behind him.

Ludik: So he kept going up?

Jonald: Well when death is behind you, you try everything to stop it in any way possible.

Soldiers came back and told them that Rio is in his house and refuse to come with them. Jonald and Ludik saddled up and went to his house. They got off of their horses in front of his house, Jonald kicked the door open and they both went in. A sword came right for them. They both moved from their places and sword missed. They saw Rio shirtless and holding the sword.

Jonald: Easy Rio, we just want to talk.

Rio looked at him and then Ludik. Rio put his sword away.

Rio: could have knocked.

Ludik moved a chair and sat on it, Rio sat on his bed while Jonald said.

Jonald: We going on a mission, you are coming with us.

Rio laughed.

"Does not look this way" Jonald smiled and said.

Jonald: We need a man who knows mountain, you went their right.

Rio: I Know, I went there when your soldiers could not.

Jonald: Well we need to go up there again.

Rio: Well everybody who goes there die, so I will stay away from there.

Jonald and Ludik looked at each other.

Ludik: We will give you one sack of gold.

Rio: No.

Ludik: I can arrest you.

Rio: For what?

Ludik: Jonald told me you are an assassin.

Rio: So? He cannot arrest me until I have committed a crime in the grassy plains or he have a proof that I killed someone in anywhere in Land of Draound.

Ludik: We can kill you, or beat you up and take you with us tied.

Rio: Try to kill me and see what happens, second thing if you take me there forcefully, who can guarantee that I will take you to the right way?

Jonald looked at Ludik and said.

Jonald: Get up, Rio is right...we cannot trust him if we take him forcefully. I Know someone else who can take us up there.

Ludik asked him while standing up.

Ludik: Who is that?

Jonald: Red shadow.

Ludik and Jonald came out. Ludik said.

"Where he lives?"

"I don't know, he has killed so much that we are ordered to kill him on sight. No proof needed, nor have been found yet"

"So why you said that"

"just wait and watch Rio come"

Jonald smiled and they heard Rio calling them. They turned around and saw Rio standing. He walked near them and said.

Rio: Two bags of gold.

Jonald: OK. Get your stuff and meet us at the castle in half an hour.

They both got up in their horse and Ludik asked Jonald.

"How did you know he will come?"

Jonald laughed and started to tell him about Rio and Red.

Soldiers and Elf walked till evening, they did not take any stop at noon, it was almost dusk and they reached to the same pond where they were yesterday. At pond they saw a weird thing. It was two feet high, its body was like a frog and also its face looked like a frog but it was walking on two feet like humans. A water ring was circulating on his head in the air. Captain ordered them to stay hidden. This frog drank some water from the pond and started to walk towards the trees. A soldier said.

Soldier: Captain, allow me to kill it.

Captain: I don't know, it is not hurting us.

Soldier: All people in the Draound will be so shocked, come on captain.

Elf looked at them and said.

Elf: It's a kappa, if it even sees a naked dagger in your hand, it will kill you. I have seen them kill big gorillas in second.

Captain looked at soldier and signaled him to stand down. They decided to spend the night near the pond. They broke many tree branches and placed some rocks together, they managed to make a wall to keep fire light as much contained as possible, they decided that if they hear see the beast they will use fire against him, Soldier formed a defensive parameter. Sun goes down and moon came up, forest went darker and darker. Captain lighted a fire and was sitting and keeping an eye on the Elf. Captain untied her and she started eating fruits, He asked her.

"What is your name?"

She did not answer.

"You will not co-operate? Already your crimes are so high"

"What crimes?"

"You killed soldiers and children"

Elf looked at him surprised.

"I did not kill anyone"

"Soldiers and Kids disappeared near the forest, that's why we came here to investigate, that's why that assassin was taking you to grassy plains"

"I do not know anything about that"

"So you are saying you have not done any of those things?"

"Yes, I live too deep in forest, I never come here"

"Are there anymore like you?" "No I am the only one"

"Any other who can do this?"

"No, small animals only go there, Beasts live deep in forest"

Suddenly they saw a small bright light in the trees. Soldier on that side looked at captain.

Elf: It's a kappa, remain calm and don't fear it nor show any aggression"

Soldier stood straight, Kappa came out of the trees, it was walking slowly like an old man, and water ring on his head was emitting light. Kappa came in front of the soldier and looked at him. Soldier stood straight. Kappa kept looking then it started walking towards the pond. Captain and Elf kept looking at it. Kappa came near them and walked past them from between them. Captain asked the Elf.

"What are they?"

"I don't know, I just saw them moving around here and there in the forest, they never posed a threat and always seemed calm, but when they feel danger, I have seen them killing animals which twenty men can not kill".

Kappa started drinking water. Then it walked back to the trees and its light faded.

Captain stared at Elf, He has seen some beautiful girls in his life but an elf beats them all. He stared at her face and forgot that she is his prisoner. Elf felt the heat of his eyes and she wrapped her arms around her. Captain felt that nothing was as pure as her face, her face looked so innocent in the golden light of the fire. Captain closed his eyes and shook his head. Elf knew that her beauty has impressed captain. Captain spoke again.

"I think you need to sleep, tomorrow you meet our Lord"

Elf opened her mouth to say something but their wall fell down all of a sudden. They saw Red standing with his sword in his hand, His sword was dripping blood. Captain jumped up but Red's punch knocked him out. Red grabbed elf's arm and picked her upon his shoulder.

She Yelled and resisted but Red's grip was too tight. Other soldiers heard her and ran towards them. Red was running fast in the forest and soldiers stopped near their captain, they did not want to go in the forest in the dark. All they could do was hear to the voice of the elf which was fading away fast. Red was running, elf's hand got touched with his dagger; she quickly pulled it out but before she could hit him, Red threw her off of his shoulder.

She fell down and tried to get up. As she got up she saw nothing around her, Red has disappeared in the dark, She turned around and saw a Kappa standing. Kappa was looking at her and her dagger. Kappa's bright light was turning brighter and it was stepping and taking a attacking stance.

She became very afraid, she looked at Kappa and then at her holding the dagger. Elf quickly threw the dagger on the ground, Kappa did not stopped walking towards her, then it stopped for a second and jumped at her making a loud squeaking noise. She closed her eyes in fear. But before Kappa could reach her, Red's sword hit him in mid air. Kappa's head got cut off clean and its body fell on the ground shaking. Water on his head stopped emitting light and fell on the ground. She opened her eyes and saw Red picking up his dagger. He turned and said to her.

"I do not want to hurt you, but you are pushing me"

She was in shock and just looked at him.

He said.

"Now will you try anything stupid again?"

She shook her head in negative, still she had a terrified look on her face.

Red tied her hands behind her back with his belt, picked her up on his shoulder again and started running. After some time she fell asleep on his shoulder.

She woke up in the morning, she was on her tree and she was tied again. She sat up and saw Red sitting in her bed, Red was without his armor and a big wound could be seen on his chest.

He must have got this in last night's fight with the soldiers. He was trying to sew it back. He saw her and said.

Red: Good morning, how are we feeling today?

Elf: What is wrong with you humans? Why you all are after me?

Red: Well killing is a crime and we humans punish criminals.

Elf: I told that soldier yesterday and I am telling you too, I did not kill any soldiers or children, I don't even go to that side of the forest.

Red stopped and looked at her.

"So you are saying that you have nothing to do with the killings?"

"That's what I am saying"

"But I heard you telling you that soldier that you live in this forest and I have seen no one except you, who can be behind this?"

"Listen shadow, I am not a killer"

"if soldiers told you my name then they must have also told you that I do not get convinced so easy"

"What I have to do then? To make all of you leave me alone"

"Give me information"

"Ask away"

"Did you kill anyone?"

"No"

"Is there anybody else in this forest that is like you or us?"

"No"

"What was that frog thing which I killed yesterday?"

"That was a Kappa, they roam in the forest"

"Why it was trying to kill you?"

"It saw your dagger in my hand, when they feel danger then they are unstoppable"

Red left the sewing and sat up, needle hanged with his wound.

"Are there any more beings that can kill or silently pick soldiers, I have seen that beast and it cannot do anything silently"

"There are no other beings in this part of the forest that have anything against humans. Wild animals even that beast does not go near the human houses, Forest side facing your homes only have small animals, which can not hurt anyone"

Red picked up an apple and bites it.

"I don't have anything against you but this is not enough information"

Elf smiled a little and said

"You mean not enough to please your lord?"

Red smiled too and said.

"I don't have a Lord, if someone needs my help, they pay me and I get the work done perfectly"

"Release me then, I have given you information"

"Not enough but now you are useless to me"

Red stood up and cut her vines. She started rubbing her arms because vines caused rashes. Red sat back in her bed and again tried to sew his wound. He said.

"You don't mind me staying here till noon, right? Those soldiers would be returning to the grassy plains and I will not get in trouble"

Elf nodded and said.

"By the way, thank you for saving me from Kappa, although you were kidnapping me"

Red laughed and tried to complete sewing his wound.

Elf: where did you get this thread and that small dagger?

Red: In my profession I could need medical attention anytime so I keep it with me all time and it is called a needle.

Elf looked at the needle again and said

"Neeedle"

Then Red sat back and Elf ate some apples and drank water. She kept looking at Red. She wanted to ask him many things about the outside world but she was a little confused and nervous. She still did not trust him completely. But it seemed like he trust him completely.

She went to stream just to check if he says anything but he did not say anything and when she came back and saw that he was laying eyes closed in her bed. She picked up her sword and unsheathed it but he did not have any reaction. He kept his eyes closed and was humming a tune.

She picked up his sword but still no response. She was still not satisfied but what could she do till noon. So she went out to pick some fruits. She picked her basket and came down. She started walking towards the trees, apple trees were a little far from her tree so she knew if he does not trust her, he will come looking for her. She took her time picking apples and bananas.

In this whole time she kept thinking if he is trustable but she did not know when she started to think about his face and a smile kept dancing on her face. After sometime she noticed this change of thoughts and she laughed on herself. While coming back to her tree she saw one of her traps. She laid many of them all around to catch small animals. A jackalope was caught in her trap. She quickly grabbed it by its horns and took It out of the trap and carried it with her on the tree. She saw Red still in the bed and humming the same tune. She said.

"Can you kill this? We can have a good lunch"

Red opened his eyes and his eyes kept getting wider.

"What is that?" he said while looking at the animal she carried. He sat up.

"I don't know, I don't have a name for it. It gives eating"

Red has never seen this animal. It was a jackrabbit with antelope horns on his head. She handed it to Red and Red grabbed it by horns. He was still in shock and rabbit was making noises and struggling to get away.

"It is a rabbit but with.....horns"

Elf placed the fruit basket in a corner and turned to him.

"Raabut?"

"Rabbit, but it has horns"

"They always have horns"

"No they don't"

"Yes they do, I have never seen any of them without horns"

Red looked at her and then jackalope and then said.

"Is it safe to eat?"

"I have been eating them since my childhood"

Red picked up his dagger and took it to the stream, Elf removed her stash of canteens, a stone platform and some square shaped stones appeared. This was her cooking station. She could not go down so she had one up here. After some-time Red came up with a skinned jackalope in his hand. She started to make a fire.

10

Chapter 10

Jonald and ludik were riding with their men, Rio was riding beside them and they just reached mountains. They past the patrols appointed from Lord Artis and after seeing Jonald they allowed to go forward. After a while of riding in the stony passage way, they started ride on the way leading up to the mountain. They could only hear their horses' breath and sound of their hooves hitting the ground.

Trees and bushes were covering all ground around them. Wind was howling and started to get colder. No one was talking bedsides ludik and Jonald; they were getting along just fine. Their voices and laughs were echoing in the mountains. Rio was leading the way and he sometimes look back at them. He was keeping a very sharp eye around his surroundings. Ludik was telling Jonald about Lord Philip and him when they got in a quarrel and Lord Philip two men with his bare hands. Rio listened and said.

Rio: I don't believe it.

Ludik; Excuse me?

Rio: Lord Philip is a great warrior but killing two men with bare hands between a fight with seven men. Really?

Ludik: He punched one man in the neck, his neck broke. That's one then he banged one man's head on the stone bench so hard that his head got crushed. I have seen it with my own eyes boy.

Rio: Who said I think you are telling the truth.

Jonald sensed that situation might go out of hands so he interrupted.

Jonald: Ludik speaks truth, he is a great warrior too.

Ludik: He would not know, there is a difference between a warrior and a coward in the shadows.

Rio just laughed and kept on going. Jonald took a breath of relief. They kept riding till night and it was the coldest night any of them ever have spent. In the morning, they started riding again, now the way or signs of way which they were following, they disappeared and now they were depending on Rio.

Rio leads them and they rode till night. All day they kept their eyes on the surroundings but nothing unusual happened. They rode the next full day and all they found were some bones. They could not tell that if they were killed by an attack or froze to death. At noon they had to leave their horses because they could not go more up so they kept on going on foot, Cold was increasing every minute they rode towards the top.

At after noon they reached the top. Jonald looked back towards the grassy plains and he was stunned by the beauty of it. He could see all the grassy plains also the Vastness of Blue Forest. Ludik tapped his shoulder and walked towards the other end. From there, they saw brown wasteland. As far as their eyes could see, there was just wasteland with some mountains in middle. They could see terrain and it was telling them that there is no good life there or maybe there is no life at all. They started to look around; on the top they did not find anything.

They came back from the top and found a level surface to make camp; they investigated area but could not find anything there too. They made the camp. There was still one or two hours left in the sunset. Jonald saw Rio standing on the side and looking at the wasteland. Jonald walked up to him and Rio said.

"If you keep walking, from this side you can reach those wastelands and if you walk to our right side you can find your way to another mountain. One day walk maximum. My father told me that that mountain is full of natural caves."

Jonald looked at the right side and said.

"We do not have time to investigate those caves, food and water will run out"

Ludik joined them and said.

Ludik: Where did you catch that thief boy?"

Rio: We are near the top, I caught him in the middle.

Jonald: What did you do to him?

Rio: Threw him in a hole.

Ludik: Why did you returned? You could have sold it.

Rio: Crown was made of some gold, not very expensive. Crowns run in families so they are more of a symbol or whatever. That reward helped me buy my house and everything. Before that I slept in taverns.

A soldier came to inform them that Dinner was ready so they all walked towards camp.

As soon as the sunset, environment got cold and they had to go into their tents.

Camp went silent. At some time in the night, Jonald woke up, He saw Rio shaking his foot and saw Ludik standing behind him. Rio put his fingers on his lips signaling Jonald to stay quiet, Jonald came out and Ludik pointed to one side. Jonald Saw a huge shadow in the corner of the camp.

Sounds were echoing in the camp, Sounds like eating and small grunts could be heard. Jonald tried to walk to get closer but Ludik stopped him and pointed in another direction. Jonald saw one more shadow walking towards the first one. Heavy footsteps could be heard.

Rio had gathered all the man from their tents, he came to Jonald and whispered

"They are eating our watchmen, let's get out of here before they see us"

They all silently walked back and as soon as they walked out of the camp, they started running.

After two hours sun came up and they took a stop to catch their breath. All soldiers were scared.

Soldier: What the hell was that?

Rio: I don't know, but they ate our men.

Ludik: I think, we have seen ogres.

All men went silent.

Jonald: I think so too, they walked like us and huge body indicates that.

Rio: Ogres are just stories. May be they are gorillas or something.

Ludik: When was the last time you seen a gorilla eat a human?

Rio looked at him. Jonald stood up:

"We must go; we need to find the horses too".

They all stood up and walked.

At the grassy plains, Lord Artis and Lord Philip were sitting in Lord Philip's camp, Lord Philip came to visit his soldiers and Lord Artis accompanied him, Soldiers were very happy that Lord Philip was between them. Lord Philip was roasting a goat, they were sitting around a fire and Lord Artis was sitting with them. A young Soldier came to Lord Philip. He had black hair with brown skin. Lord Philip saw him and yelled.

Lord Philip: Hey! Look who is here.

All soldiers raised their glasses and cheered. Young Soldier bowed to them while smiling.

Lord Philip put his arm around him and took him in front of Lord Artis.

Lord Philip: I want you to meet Lord Artis, our host and Lord of beautiful grassy plains.

Soldier bowed and said

"My lord"

Lord Philip then said.

Lord Philip: Lord Artis meet Herald; he is one of my best fighters.

Lord Artis raised his glass.

Lord Philip: Some say he is even a greater warrior then Ludik.

Lord Artis: We should hold a match between them.

Herald smiled and said

"My Lords, Ludik is a far greater warrior then me"

Lord Philip gave him a glass of wine and said

"Hahaha, he is just being modest, now come we have meat and wine"

They all laughed and they all sat together. Lord Phillip said

Lord Phillip: You know, Herald saved me three times in fights.

Lord Artis: Well I cannot say if you need any help in fighting.

Lord Philip laughed and said.

"A dead fighter is not a great fighter; all great fighters are backed up by their comrades who save them from an early death"

Herald smiled and raised his glass and shouted.

"TO LORD PHILLIP"

All soldiers raised their glasses and cheered.

Elf and Red were sitting on her tree, bones of Jackalope were lying in front of them, and they have just eaten lunch. Red was thinking about what to do next because he knew that soldiers are looking for them. He could not go into the forest to face them, he would be fighting them and also watch his back for beasts and Kappas and what not. He looked at the Elf who was checking his sword. He said.

"Can I go around the soldiers?"

Elf looked at him and said

"What do you mean?"

"I mean from the area which we came, they must be looking for us and if I go head on, I would be fighting with them and also fight those forest animals.

" Well, you can easily do that, I can tell you the way but you have to look out for the beasts, they are always moving in the forest, Forest was quite peaceful before they came to these parts"

"What derived them from the deep forest parts?"

"I don't know"

"Do you know what lives in the deep forest?"

"No, we moved here when I was little"

"We?"

Elf looked at him and looked down again

"You must be going, noon is here"

"I cannot, I must go to deeper parts of the forest"

"You will die"

"I took a job, I must do it completely"

"So you can please your lord?"

"this is my only choice"

"Soldier said that you kill people for money"

"Yes, I am best at what I do"

"Why are you leaving me alive?"

"Why would I kill you?"

"I don't know, you were sent here to deal with the one who is responsible? But you did not kill me instead you captured me."

"I was sent here to investigate, I thought you were the one killing all the people, if I killed you and just went back and told them that I killed the responsible person, they would ask for a proof. I cannot take your dead body to that far with all those animals in the forest"

"Now you are going in the deep forest, why?"

"If I go now and someone again got disappeared, I would be accused of not completing the deal, rewards will be taken away and my name in my profession will be defamed "

Elf smiled and said

"I did not think that a killer would care for his name being defamed"

"When people want people dead, they want surety that it is done right and if someone knows that I did not complete job, they will start to give jobs to other paid killers meaning I will lose money"

"So that's what makes Shadow the top killer?"

"Yes"

"You can go back and tell them about me"

"No one will believe that an Elf is alive, also no one will come in the Blue Forest".

"You did"

Red laughed and said

"Because I saw you on the edge of the forest"

"What is stopping you from tying me again and taking to your Lord?"

"You said you have nothing to do with killings, plus with those soldiers lurking in the forest I would not be able to take you silently"

Elf smiled. Red was right with all those soldiers and those beasts, Red could try all his tricks but either Elf could do a lot of things to give up their position and Red could not carry her fast enough to make it out of the Forest. Red stood up and started putting on his armor. Red sheathed his sword and stood up.

Red wore his sword and dagger. He tied his belt, his belt had little pocket on its back in which Red kept his medic kit. Red picked up an apple and a canteen then asked her about the way. She told him the way to the deep forest. Red started climbing down the tree and after reaching the ground, he started walking towards the stream, after crossing it he disappeared in the trees. Elf sat down and started thinking about her past days.

In the Forest, Soldiers were looking for them. Captain was so angry because Red killed his three soldiers last night and then he took their prisoner from right in front of their eyes, they searched the area in which direction they went, they found the body of a beheaded Kappa.

Then they looked for foot prints and such signs like pressed bushes or blood drops from Red's sword or any wound he bore. They found some signs and started following them. Because Red was running in the night and also he had Elf on his shoulder, Bushes were pressed hard under his feet and he also broke branches from small trees. They followed those signs till evening. They heard the roaring of the Beasts several times in the whole day. They would become more careful every time they heard the beast. In the afternoon they reached a dead end, they could find no signs.

They started sweeping the area but could not find anything, they felt a little down but after half an hour they found a broken canteen. Captain ordered them to move into that direction. After a little walking they found a stream. Now this was an open area, they could not just walk right across it because any beast or may be Red could see them.

Captain ordered them to first recon the other bank carefully and do it while as hidden as possible. They started moving hidden along the bank of the stream. One soldier whistled,

Captain looked at him and he pointed across the stream, They saw the Elf coming with some cloths.

She sat on the bank of the stream and started rinsing her cloths, Captain recognized the cloths, and those were deer skins which she was wearing when they captured her, now she was wearing black colored clothing which must be black deer skin. Captain whistled and all his soldiers looked at him, he signaled them to stay put. He signaled one soldier to come to him. Soldier came near him and Captain said.

Captain: She is washing clothes, which mean she lives nearby. We will wait for dusk then cross the stream. Pass it to others.

Soldier nodded and went back to tell others. They knew it was only two hours till dusk but beast roams this area so they had to watch their backs too. After one hour sun started to set and forest turned dark. Insect's voices started to rise. Chirping and sometimes owl's hooting made the Forest a little spookier.

Captain waited for fifteen minutes more and when darkness fell completely, they crossed the stream. They made no sound while crossing, Soldier kept the track of the path by which Elf left so they found the path easily. But now they did not know what to do. They could see no house or hut, not even a fire which could show that someone lives there. Captain whispers in the soldier's ear.

Captain: Don't make any sound, stay put and let me think. May be we have to make a camp here.

Soldier whispered this command to other soldier and he passed that to another. Now they were all standing in the dark and waiting for Captains command. Suddenly a soldier heard something, sounded like a faint humming. He silently reached the captain and whispered the information in his ear. Captain and all soldiers held their breaths and tried to listen to the humming. They heard a very faint humming.

They started moving around to see from which direction the sound was coming from but every time they went away from their original position the sound went fainter. In all the voices of the Forest it was very hard to listen to the voice. Captain looked up and saw square shaped shadow.

Trees are not square and a smile spread on his face. He whispered to the soldier about the location of the Elf. Captain and soldiers gathered around the tree trunk and felt some carvings in the trunk. A soldier tried to climb but Captain stopped him. Soldier armor and sword would make sound. He ordered them to stay put and wait. Humming stopped and after almost one hour of waiting, Captain started climbing with soldiers following him.

On the mountains, Jonald and his comrades had reached their horses and now they were riding towards the grassy plains. They all were thinking about reaching grassy plains as fast as they can. Jonald instructed them to not to tell anyone until they talk to Lord Artis. It could spread chaos. Ludik and Rio were riding behind him. They lost 2 soldiers last night and right now they were thinking about that if they should make camp.

Ludik: I can ride all night.

Rio sarcastically said: You can, but we are not great warriors like you. We will need rest and horses will too.

Jonald: We left all our stuff at the top.

Rio: I am only saying that we will need rest.

Ludik: What if those things come down here.

Rio: You will be eaten alive but they did not come when we made camp two days ago.

Jonald: they did not know that we were there but now they may follow us.

Ludik: So we ride through the night?

Jonald: Yes.

And they kept on riding.

11

CHAPTER 11

Something hit Captain on the face hard, He opened his eyes because of pain but instead of his home, he saw trees and an Elf reaching for a sword in the corner. His mind recalled all the past days and within one second he understood the situation. He shouted while standing up.

"Wake up you idiots"

Elf quickly turned around and her face showed that she was angry. All soldiers woke up and reached for their swords. Elf quickly picked her sword up and unsheathed it. A soldier struck her; she blocked it and moved to the right. Another soldier struck her but she dodged it and turned her body in circle with cutting soldiers throat with her sword, once again she was pointing her sword towards them. Captain only had three soldiers left. He swung his sword at her feet but she blocked and struck his hand from side of the sword. Captain grunted and his sword fell down, Elf quickly came at his back and put her sword on his neck.

Elf: Don't move or your captain will die.

Soldier stopped and looked at them. Captain's face showed anger.

Elf: Now Captain, order your soldiers to throw their swords down and you take me down this tree.

Captain: Throw down the swords.

Soldiers threw their swords down, captain and elf backed up slowly till they reached the trunk. Elf put her legs around his waist with her sword still at his throat. Captain started climbing down the trunk. Soldiers saw them going down. When they reached a third way down, Captain Let the trunk go. Elf screamed and Captain grabbed her arm keeping her at his back. Elf fell and on her the captain. Soldiers picked up their swords and started climbing down, Captain quickly took her sword, Elf face showed a lot of pain and she was holding her knee. Captain pointed her sword at her. Soldiers reached down and one of them gives captain back his sword.

Soldier: I think she broke her leg.

Captain: I don't care, she killer one of our man.tie her up.

Soldiers tied her hands and feet with their belts and one of them picked her up on his shoulders. They started walking from where they came from, across the stream and to the same pond where they found them in the first place. Captain pulled her hair and said.

"Tell me where to go"

Elf said nothing. Captain looked at her face and punched her on her damaged knee.

Elf yelled due to pain, her voice echoed in the Forest.

Captain: I will do it again, if you do not speak and if this time we get lost, I will break your other leg too and then drag you till I see grassy plains.

Elf started crying; Captain raised his hand and punched her knee again. She yelled like before and captain asked again. She told him in which direction to go. They started walking and captain warned her again and again. At noon they reached the place where they were attacked by Forest Dogs. Captain and Soldiers became happy and started walking fast. They took no rest and near dusk they were out of the

Forest, they walked out of the Forest and could see the valley houses and castle. There was no patrol around but they did not have that in mind and they started walking towards the valley. Darkness was spreading but now they were out of the Forest so they were not worried, they could see the fires burning in the houses and market across the plain. All they had to do was to walk across this plain which was covered with grass. Captain looked at his soldier and said

"Finally, I am walking on ground which is not blue"

Soldiers laughed, Elf said nothing. They kept on walking and their faces turned more relax. They all were very happy and talking about how Lord Phillip will react when he sees the Elf. Ground took a slope; They walked down the slope and then walked up. Soldier carrying the Elf slipped and fell. Elf gasped as her bad leg just hit the ground. All men looked at him and laughed. One soldier yelled

"Get up, we are almost home"

But the Soldier did not move. Captain walked down to him while saying

"We all are tired but we have to reach the houses"

Captain shook his arm, he did not move. Captain pulled his arm but felt that he is not even trying to get up. Captain turned him over and he heard thudding behind him. He turned around and saw both of his remaining soldiers lying on the ground and slipping on the slope. He got shocked and he started running up, he climbed the slope and saw a patrol and he yelled.

"Hey, hey.... i need help over here"

Someone pulled him back and he fell on the slope, he saw a shadow and heard a voice.

"Good night Captain"

It was Red's voice, Captain recognized him without any mistake but before he could say anything, Red stabbed him in the heart. Red quickly got up and ran to the Elf. He saw the patrol turning this way. He only had three darts that gave the Captain chance to run. Red already took out the darts from the necks of the soldiers and now he was picking up the Elf. Elf resisted but Red said.

"It's me, Shadow"

Elf calmed down after knowing that it was Red. Red picked her up on his shoulder and ran towards the curve of the slope. Before patrolmen could come he was running towards the houses from far left of that location. After reaching the houses, he went in the empty streets. He was moving to a safe house. He owned a house in this valley about which no one knew. After some hiding and running he reached his house. It was a warehouse. Its front gate was always locked because he always uses backdoor. Red opened the backdoor and took the Elf inside. After reaching in he locked the door from inside and took the Elf to another room. In this room there was a bed, he put her there and untied her. She was in pain. Red lighted a torch, Elf saw that this room had no window; A hole in the roof was giving the fresh air. Elf said

"My knee is broken"

"I know but I cannot take you anywhere right now, whole army will be looking for us now"

"I want to go back to the Forest"

"We will, but right now we cannot"

Red stood up and went to a corner. There was a table with many jars on it. Red started making some medicine. After a while Red came back to her. He gave him some herbs folded in a big leaf.

"Eat this, it will make you sleep so you will not feel pain....i will see what I can do for your knee"

Elf ate the leaf and herbs. Red went back to the table and started mixing things again. After some minutes she felt her head spinning and she closed her eyes to sleep.

When she woke up, she saw herself in a bed and an old woman dressing her knee. She quickly got up but a shooting pain in her knee made her stop. The old woman looked at her and said.

"Calm down young one, your knee is just fractured, it is not broken"

Elf looked at her terrified, she asked

"Where am i?"

Before she could answer, door opened and Renald entered.

"You are awake? Very good"

Old woman got up and left while Renald went to study table and started writing something on the pad. Elf looked around the room but could not see much as it was dark and she had tears in her eyes because of pain, in the whole room only one torch was lit. She tried to move her leg, it was paining but less then yesterday. She felt something around her head. She touched her head and found that a scarf was covering her head along with her pointy ears. She was still trying to figure out where is she and where is Red then she heard some footsteps. Door opened and Lord Artis entered. Lord Artis looked at the room then turned to Renald and said.

"You idiot, I invited that idiot Phillip here, luckily he had no interest investigating a woman"

Red came out of a dark corner. Renald opened his mouth but Lord Artis did not let him speak. He asked Red. "What's the matter? And who is this woman"

Elf saw Red, she felt relaxed a little bit but she knew she cannot tell about her being an elf.

Elf: I am a human.

Lord Artis and Renald looked at her then at Red.

Elf: I mean I live in this valley, in the last homes.

Lord Artis: So? What you doing in my castle.

Elf: Some soldiers attacked me last night, Shadow saved me.

Lord Artis and Renald had a surprised reaction on their face, Lord Artis said to Red.

"You? Saved someone?"

Elf: Yes, he saved me and he took m....

But before she could end her sentence, Red pulled her scarf off of her head. Lord Artis and Renald got shook. They could not believe their eyes, there was a living Elf in front of them. Lord Artis opened his mouth to say something but could not say anything. Red went to a chair and sat on it. He looked at them both and said.

"There is your killer"

Elf saw him in surprise but before she could say anything, Lord Artis spoke.

"Wha....wai....what...what..what do you ....what do you mean?"

"found her in the Forest, Only human like creature in the whole Forest"

Elf could not believe that Red betrayed her.

Lord Artis: You found her in the Forest?

Red: Yes.

Renald: How did you capture her?

Red: Punched her.

Lord Artis came close and touched her ear to make sure they were real, she slapped away his hand and Lord Artis said.

"Are there anymore?"

Red: No, I made sure of it.

Lord Artis: Is that why you took so many days?

Red: Yes but also Lord Phillip's men made some trouble.

Renald: Lord Phillip is angry with you, his soldiers were found dead in the valley near the houses, black Fry was found to be the cause of death.

Red smiled and said.

"Yeah, I could not carry her with them lurking in the Forest, so I took their help"

Elf looked at Red. She could not believe what she was hearing.

Lord Artis: And you killed them when they carried her to the valley?"

"Yes, or else they would take her to Phillip"

Elf spoke in sadness.

"I should have killed you when I had the chance"

Lord Artis looked at Red confused. Red lifted his shoulder up.

Lord Artis smiled and looked at her knee.

"What happened to her leg?"

"Accident while Phillip's men were trying to arrest her, your idiot manager called a doctor to dress her wound, luckily her head was covered or else she would know"

Lord Artis looked angrily at Renald. Renald gulped. Red stood up and took out his dagger.

"Well I think it is time"

Elf looked at him terrified, she said.

"I did not kill anyone, I did not kill anybody"

Red took steps towards her and Lord Artis said.

"In bed? Are you serious? My sheets will be all bloody"

Red look at him and pulled her from the arm, she fell down from the bed. She yelled again.

"Please listen to me, I did not kill anyone...it must be something from the deep forest"

Lord Artis looked at Red and Red looked at him. Red put his dagger on her neck and said.

"What do you mean?"

"I don't know, I don't know"

Lord Artis: She is speaking nonsense.

Elf: No, I am telling the truth... I heard loud noises from those parts.

Lord Artis: What noises?

But elf was out of breath and could not answer.

Lord Artis yelled: What noises?

Elf gasped. Renald looked at them both and said.

"My Lord, if I may?"

Lord Artis looked at him and Red left her arm while putting his dagger away. Renald came forward and sat her up on bed. Lord Artis gave Red a meaningful smile. Renald spoke.

"Relax, no one is going to hurt you....shhh..shhh"

Red face palmed himself while Lord Artis laughed silently. Renald kept Talking.

"don't worry, everything will be fine. First you need to stop crying"

Elf tried to stop sobbing. Red poured some wine and came close to them while holding his wine glass in front and said.

"Perhaps a beverage will help"

Lord Artis started laughing in the back, Renald took the glass and gave it to the elf, Red went back and poured some more wine in another glass. Elf took a sip and she spits it all out. Renald looked into the glass then at Red and Red just lifted his shoulders. Lord Artis poured some water in a water glass, he picked it and came close to them and said

"May be this kid wants some water"

Renald took it and Lord Artis went back smiling. Renald gave the Elf water and she drank the whole glass. Renald kept comforting her, when stopped sobbing he said.

"Tell us what to do you know about the killer?"

She did not say anything.

"Look, we don't have anything against you....we just want to catch the murderer who killed innocent people"

Red looked at Lord Artis sarcastically and Lord Artis started drinking wine while smiling. After some time they heard her voice.

"I do not know, I never saw anyone"

"Anything you know?"

"I moved from the deep forest when I was a kid, I started living on the tree where I live now. For some weeks, beasts from the deep forest started to come to my part of the Forest, they never come here. And i..i hear..."

"What do you hear?"

"I hear loud voices from those parts. Not like humans or elves or anything I have ever heard"

"You ever went to see what is there?"

"No, that place is lurking with so many dangerous animals that no one can take ten steps without fighting something, but I saw big beasts coming from those parts with fresh big wounds"

Renald looked at Lord Artis, Lord Artis looked at Red, Red put down his glass, stood up, set his armor then he took out his dagger.

"No,,, what are you doing?" Lord Artis yelled.

Red: What?

Renald came to the table and pour some more water and gave it to the Elf.

Renald: are you hungry?

Elf: no.

Renald: Don't worry, no one will hurt you, are you hungry.

Elf nodded in yes and Renald went to kitchen to get some food for her. Red and Lord Artis kept staring at her and sipping wine. Elf looked at Red and her eyes filled with anger, Lord Artis looked at them both and said.

Lord Artis: Did anything happened?

Red: What you mean?

Lord Artis: I mean Physical, anything physical happened between you two.

Red: No!

Lord Artis: Why she looking at you like that, so much anger.

Red: trusted me.

Lord Artis: Oh, fool.

Renald returned with some bread and meat in a dish. He handed the dish to Elf and she started eating.

Red: So now we feeding her, that means we are not killing her, right?

Lord Artis: Why kill her, she gave us some important information, she can help us more.

Red looked disappointed. While Elf kept on eating.

After two hours Lord Artis came into the room with Red and Renald, Elf was lying in the bed.

She looked at them, Renald stood in a corner, Lord Artis stood in front of the bed while Red went to a chair and sat. Lord Artis spoke.

Lord Artis: I have an offer for you.

Elf looked at him, he added

Lord Artis: I want you to investigate the deep parts of the Forest and then report back to me. I can pay you in gold.

Renald: My lord, she lives in the forest, I do not think gold will be of any value to her.

Lord Artis: hmmm, you can come live here in the valley, no one will make you uncomfortable and you will be one of the richest.

Elf: I will not work for you.

Lord Artis: Is this your final answer?

Elf: Yes.

Lord Artis looked disappointed and he said.

Lord Artis: Ok then.

There was a knock on the door. Renald opened it a little and a servant gave him some stuff, he closed the door and turned around. He was holding cloths.

Lord Artis: This Is a gift from me. Some fine cloths for a fine lady like you.

Renald put the cloths on bed near the elf. These were leather made cloths.

Lord Artis: I would have got you a dress but after hearing Red, I don't think dress was your type.

Renald: These will do great in hunting and moving fast.

Elf: You are not killing me?

Lord Artis laughed while Renald smiled.

Lord Artis: Why would i? I do not want to waste such a beauty.

Elf felt a little relaxed. Renald gazed at her.

Lord Artis: If you ever need anything my castle doors are always open for you, just two things.

Elf: What?

Lord Artis: You have to guide Red to the Deep Forest.

Elf: Who is Red?

Lord Artis pointed at Red.

Elf: His name is Shadow.

Renald: He has many names.

Elf: why?

Lord Artis: not important.

Elf: Second?

Lord Artis: You see anything unusual in....

Lord Artis stopped and looked at her and then he again said

"Anything related to the killings, you report them to me... Not as a service but for the innocent people of Grassy Plains."

Elf: I will do it, but no one will bother me in the forest, ever again.

Lord Artis: Done.

Elf: and I will kill Red, first chance I get.

Lord Artis: You are welcome to but just guide him to the deep forest first.

Elf nodded. Lord Artis looked at Red. He was scratching wine glass with his dagger.

Renald: Anything else you need?

Elf: A sword, like this idiot has.

Lord Artis looked at Red's sword and said

Lord Artis: Give her your sword.

Red: Hell with that.

Renald: Mind your language; you are in presence of a Lord.

Red: wanna kiss my fist?

Lord Artis: just give her your sword, I will give you another one.

Red: I forged this sword by my own hands, get her a new one.

Lord Artis: seriously?

Red: Yup.

Lord Artis: well.

He unsheathed his sword, looked at it and then sheathed it.

Lord Artis: You can have this one, it was forged by best sword maker of Kashfin, it is light as a feather and specially made for fighting in close quarters, as Lords get ambushed in their halls and castles.

Elf: I accept this one.

Lord Artis: That's it then, change your cloths and Renald will get you two horses, I will command to pull back patrols from the forest's edge.

Red stood up and they all headed out. After one hour they were standing outside the castle. Red was already gone to the forest and Lord Artis along with Renald were standing with the Elf. She was covering her ears with a scarf and was wearing the cloths Lord Artis gave her. Her new sword was hanging on the side. She sat on the horse and Lord Artis nodded at her. But before she could kick the horse. Renald came forward.

Renald: I just wanted to say that.....you know...that

Elf: What?

Renald was confused and nervous.

Renald: IF you like....if you want to ....like start a family.....i would want to be your father.....i mean your children's father.

Lord Artis covered his mouth while laughing; Elf made a very bad face and kicked the horse. Horse started running towards the town. Lord Artis came laughing to Renald and said.

"What was that?"

"I got confused, I was nervous....she is so beautiful"

"hahahaha, you need some help in these matter"

Renald sighed while Lord Artis laughed loudly and they both started walking. Elf rode through market, she saw the people, kids, men and women. She became very happy.

She saw everybody doing their work, Men at the shops, women buying from shops, kids playing and soldiers patrolling. She also saw women cleaning their houses and kids playing in front. She did not know when she was out of the houses and now was riding in the plains.

She saw the Blue Forest in front and became very sad because she lived alone for whole her life and the day she sees a human, she gets punched, kidnapped and have a fractured knee. She almost died by the hands of Red. She started thinking about him and then about his face.

She again came to her senses and could not understand what just happened to her. Her horse was running fast and she did not know and now she was reaching the Forest. She headed straight to the opening where Renald said that Red will be waiting. She stopped the horse in the forest and looked around, then she looked on the trees around but Red was not there. She heard a voice

"Let's go"

She looked in front; Red was standing near her horse.

"Where were you?"

"Why?" "Answer me"

"No need, we need to go"

He climbed on the horse behind her, She tried to say something but she could not. They rode a little but trees started narrowing. There were so many trees that horse could not go straight and had to find way.

Elf: We will never reach my house like this.

Red: Then what do you suggest.

Elf: We must go on foot.

Red: I have two good legs, you do not.

Elf: SO?

Red: SO how will we reach your place?

Elf: Carry me.

Red: I don't think so.

Elf: You did that night when you kidnapped me from those soldiers.

Red: Not today.

After some time, When horse was unable to find a way, Red agreed and they let the horse go. Elf put her arms around Red's neck and tied her legs around his waist from the back and Red started walking. He walked till noon. He took a break at noon and they sat down. Red said

"First of all, give me my dagger back and second how those soldiers caught you"

Elf threw his dagger near his feet; she took it out while he was carrying her thinking he would not know.

Elf: I do not know.

Elf thought for a moment and suddenly she said:

"They must have heard me humming, I did it without think-ing"

"Humming?"

"Yes, you were doing on that morning; I was trying to do the same"

Red laughed and Elf put her head down. After the Rest Red again carried her and at dusk they reached her tree. Red climbed the tree and laid her in her bed. Red took some fruits out of her basket and gave them to her, some he ate himself then he drank some water and gave another canteen to Elf. Elf drank the water. Red could not go to deep forest in night so he had to sleep here. Red was sitting and was sharpening his sword. Elf trusted him once but she did not want to do it again. She kept looking at him. She said.

"Don't you want to know the way?"

"You told me before, I remember everything"

"Do you remember what I told your Lord in the castle?"

"That you will kill me first chance you get?" "Yes"

"I remember"

"But still you will stay here?"

"Yes"

She took a deep breath, she was angry at him and his calmness was making her more angry. She asked

"Why? I can kill you in your sleep"

Red laughed and said

"You are too innocent, I think it is because you did not interacted with anyone in your life, now I feel bad about drugging you, I could just ask you whether you will kill me or no"

"What do you mean drugging?"

Red laughed again

"Drugging means I gave you something to put you to sleep"

"What? You did not gave me anything"

"In your water canteen, I mixed a little something when I gave it to you so now you will not be able to cause me a problem until morning"

Elf put her hand on his head, he fooled her again.

"You are evil"

Red smiled in the dark

"Thank you, I take it as a compliment"

Then Red got back to sharpening while Elf tried to stay awake but she fell asleep after sometime.

12

Chapter 12

At sometime before dawn, A servant woke up Lord Artis telling that he is needed in the throne room. When Lord Artis got there, he saw Lord Philip sitting beside throne, in front of him was standing Jonald along with his companions. Servants were giving them water. Lord Artis saw their rough condition and sat on the throne. Lord Philip said to him

"Ludik called me, I hope you do not mind"

"No problem"

Then lord Artis spoke to Jonald

"What happened? by looking at you I can tell that it is not a good news"

Jonald did a nod towards the servants and Lord Artis ordered the servants to go, After that Jonald told everything. After hearing Jonald Lord Philip said

Lord Philip: I would not believe if any other man told me all this.

Lord Artis: I still cannot believe it.

Rio: I saw the whole thing and I could not believe it while standing there.

Lord Philip: Now what to do?

Lord Artis: I will double the forces on mountain side.

Lord Philip: Can our men fight ogres? Or whatever those things are?

Lord Artis: We have to do something about it, we will see once they come down but right now no one goes up and all of you keep this to yourself.

Jonald: I have ordered these man already my lord but my lord what about the forest?

Lord Artis: Cannot say anything yet.

Ludik: What if they are in the forest too my lord? We must investigate.

Lord Artis: Remember what happened to your soldiers Ludik?

Lord Philip: People are saying my men are killed by Shadow death.

Lord Artis: You want to send more men in the Forest? I am not sending any more men there to go to waste. In that damn forest there are many things which can kill a man.

Everybody stood silent and then Lord Artis spoke

"Right now, you all can go home and take rest, at least now we know what are up against"

They all bowed and left the throne room then Lord Philip stood up and asked Lord Artis

"Now?"

"I need to see my commanders"

"I advise you to send a letter to your home too, I will do the same"

"you are right, my son always wanted to rule, I guess it is time to make him official acting Lord"

"I never met your son"

Lord Artis smiled at him and Lord Philip walked out.

In the forest, Elf woke up at dawn. She sat up in her bed and saw Red sitting with his armor on and sword lying in front of him. His eyes were looking at the rising sun and he was humming the same tune he was humming the first time she met him. He turned his head towards her and she noticed that he also just woke up. She climbed down the tree and went to stream. She washed her face and drank some water. She returned and saw Red holding her sword, he threw her sword at her and said

"Let's go"

She wore her sword and they both climbed down the tree. She walked with a little difficulty but she managed to keep walking. Red was walking very slowly because of her. They head towards toward the inner parts of the forest. They kept walking and saw some jackalopes and lemurs. They saw some gorillas and kept low until gorillas moved away. At near noon, they started to hear loud growls, with every step they were becoming louder and more frequent. Elf started to step more cautiously. At noon Elf stopped and looked at Red. Red understood that from here he have to go alone. It was an open area with a giant boulder with no trees around it. Elf said

"Go straight; this is as far as I can go"

Red walked past her and her mouth opened to say something but she did not know what to say. She stopped and saw Red disappearing in the trees. All she could see now were tree and hear Loud Growls. She knew that Red is never coming back because she knew the dangers of the forest and without even going in the inner parts she can say that it was the last time she is going to see Red. She turned around and started walking but her feet felt heavy and her heart started beating fast. She could not understand why but she became very sad. She turned one last time but could saw the same old picture. She walked back to her tree.

General Riendo and General Salvador were walking among soldiers. They have been briefed about what happened to Jonald and his venture so now they had to call every soldier in the valley on duty. They were talking about this and they saw Lord Artis and Lord Philip walking towards them. Soldiers saw two Lords among them so they bowed to them. Lord Artis said

"No need for formalities, carry on your work"

And everyone went back to what they were doing. Lord Artis asked Riendo

Lord Artis: what is the report Riendo?

Riendo: My lord, we have called every soldier in the valley.

Lord Artis: I want half of them posted near the mountains and one third part near the forest and give one third to that captain to keep peace in the valley.

Salvador: My lord, he is just a captain, by law he is not eligible to lead such big part of an army.

They saw Jonald walking with Ludik and coming towards them. They both reached them and bowed.

Lord Artis: Well let's make it official then.

They all looked at him and he added

Lord Artis: I hereby promote you to the rank of a... what must be his rank for such a job?

Salvador and Riendo looked at each other and then Riendo said

"General.... my lord, if he is to lead one third part of an army"

Lord Artis: Well I promote Jonald to the rank of General.

Soldiers listened to this and starting clapping and cheering. They all loved Jonald and past days have proved that he is a good person who loved this valley. Jonald was very confused and he asked

Jonald: My lord I am....

Lord Artis: No time..... You take one third of this army and now you are responsible for keeping peace in the valley.

Jonald knew the critical situation so he just nodded and walked off with Ludik. General Salvador and Riendo Also bowed and walked. Lord Artis started talking with Lord Philip

then they saw Renald coming to them. Renald reached them
and said

"My lord, letter from home"

Lord Artis: what does it say?

Renald: Everything is good and your instructions are in effect.

Lord Artis: Good.

Then they got back to talking about army position.

Acting Lord Brett Artis son of Lord Dake Artis. He was 28 year
old man with a big physique. He always could be seen with his
friends. He always obeyed his father and wanted to rule like
him. Brett had features like his father. When he knew that he
was the acting lord of his land, he took it very seriously and
carried out his father's commands and now was sitting in the
throne room drinking with his best friend.

Bryte was his best friend and son of a soldier. Brett used
to play with him when a kid then he joined army and Brett
took him as his personal body guard. Four days were past
since his father ordered him to strengthen up his defenses but
nothing happened. Their lands were lying with Lord Henry's
lands so they also touched the mountains but no missing
happened in their lands. They were discussing this issue and
after discussion Brett stood up, it was time for him to sleep or
else he would not be able to sit properly in throne room. His
bodyguard walked out as he walked to his sleeping chambers.

The next morning in the grassy plains, Lord Artis called Renald to see if any news from anywhere but nothing came in. Mountains were quite and it was good at home like always. For four days Red was in the Forest and has not returned. Lord Artis was starting to believe that Ogres are staying up the mountains and not coming down.

After breakfast and meeting up with Lord Philip he ordered army to loosen up the defense. All soldiers took a breath of relief because they were not told what they were up against. He called commanders to decide their next step. Lord Philip decided to take all of his men to fight on the mountain. Lord Artis went against it but now they knew what was the reason behind all this mess there was no reason for Lord Philip to stay.

Also ogres were not coming down so someone had to deal with this problem. Lord Philip was a warrior and he was thinking that killing ogres will make him most famous warrior. He ordered his men to march up the mountains. Missings at the Forest were now thought to be any beasts doings because there was no report of any more missing or sighting of anything unusual.

In the Forest, Elf was living her daily life, her knee was healed and she took many walks in the forest to look for a new location for her home. This place was now compromised and humans know about this place so she was looking for a new place. Today she was walking to the same place where she left Red.

She was thinking that humans will not come near the deep parts so let's look for a place there. After she reached that place she saw the big boulder and remembered Red. She did not want to think about him so she kept walking. After a lot of searching and looking around she did not find any suitable location so she returned. When she walked half way back, she saw someone lying on the ground. She came close and a smile appeared on her face.

She recognized the armor and she drew her sword. She came close to Red, he was lying face down, she turned him and saw his armor tore and bloody. Red eyes were closed and he had his sword in his hand. He was covered with blood. Elf smiled as it was her chance to get revenge. She raised her arm and got ready to strike.

She looked at his face and tried to swing her sword but she could not bring her arms down. She was unable to do it. Red betrayed her and tried to kill her but she could not kill him. She got ready again and tried to swing her sword but again she could not. She could not believe herself. She did it again and failed.

She did not know what was happening. She thought to herself that this is a man who put his knife on her neck but her heart said that he was doing what he was told to. She just stood there with her sword in her hand convincing herself to strike and end him but she could not. After half an hour of arguing with herself, She decided that she will just leave him here. Any animal can finish him off.

She started walking back with heavy feet but she did not stop.

13

CHAPTER 13

After three days more, Lord Philip reached the top but they did not see anything unusual in the way, they swept the whole area and after that they marched to the mountain lying beside them, there were reports of caves in it. They reached there but there were caves. Spending a whole day there sweeping the area but nothing was found. They spent the night at the top and the next day marched back.

At grassy plains, Lord Artis received a letter with all Lords signs that Lord Artis was to return to his Lands and Throne of grassy plains will be in it's army's protection until the people of grassy plains choose their own lord which may be from the common people or from any other lord of any land. Lord Artis got furious and did not want to leave but what could he do. His army was in his own land and he did not have enough time to earn Henry's army trust. He ordered his men to pack up and call all three Generals to come to castle as the protocol required and gave the crown to them. He was to evacuate the castle the next morning as a feast must be arranged in his honor to thank him for his services to the throne in the time of need, As the protocol stated.

Brett was walking to his guest chambers, he was accompanied by his two body guards. They entered the chambers and gather around the bed. On the bed someone was lying. Brett called.

"Red.. Red...wake up"

The person in the bed moved a little and after sometime sat up. It was Red. He was shirtless and his chest had too new stitched wounds and one on his arm. He looked at Brett and said

"What?"

"It is time"

Red stood up and they started walking. Red did not remember how he came here. AL he remember was when he fell unconscious after coming out of the forest and when he woke up he was in this room. He was cared for and fed. Brett came to him and told him that he was in Lord Artis castle but did not tell him how he got here. He was just told that soon he will be told and now it was time. They crossed the hall way and came into another room. In this room there was no furniture and some torches were lit with some symbols made on floor. Red looked at the symbols and asked Brett

"Now?"

Suddenly black smoke started to rise out of the ground between the symbols. Red almost jumped out of his skin. Smoke started to take the shape of a human and became a real human person. He was a normal man but different cloths which were made of wool and face features changed then them. His skin was pale and risen cheek bones. He came forward and shook hands with Brett. Then he looked at Red and raised his hand, Red shook his hand and then they all walked out. Red was still confused on what he just saw. They all reached the study and sat on the chairs around the table. Brett looked at Red and said

"Red I like you to meet our dear friend Altan"

Red looked at him and he smiled. Brett said again

"Altan, this is Red. One of the most skilled warrior in all the lands"

Altan spoke for the first time.

"Did you tell him everything?"

Brett: NO, I was waiting for you.

Altan: As you can see, I am not from your lands, I am a representative of our great king Adlard.

We live in the Cold desert of Alois beyond the clay land.

Red looked at Brett and he said

"Wastelands, he calls them clay land"

Altan: Our king comes from a great and long line of kings, his ancestors were the kings before him and use to command the desert of Alois. Alois is a place which is unique, This desert have forests in it with streams and mineral ores. Our ancestors crossed the clay lands to your lands to seek riches but one time your people fought them and derived them from your land long ago, they crossed the clay land and found nothing, just more desert but this desert was better than clay lands and they started to live there.

He took a little pause and spoke again

Atlan: When they derived our ancestors, most of our people died and rest were hunted till they found Desert of Alois and killed all our people. Only few families left who hid here and there. But now our numbers great again and Our people want revenge.

Brett: What I believe is that he is talking about the great battle of Draound.

Red: I think so too, but why we are having this conversation.

Altan: We do not want to make mistake our ancestors made, our people are not as disciplined as your army. They don't fight with co ordination. We need man who know fighting of your people's style.

You saw how I came here, right?

Red: Black magic, I figured.

Atlan: Brett thinks you are a great warrior and insists that you fight with us.

Red looked at Brett and asked

Red: Why?

Brett: I always admired you, ruthless and stone cold. Who do you think gave my father the idea of hiring you? and I know that you are not into that loyalty or care for innocent type of stuff.

Red: But what will I get?

Atlan: Everything, Share in lands and loot, we will go beyond your lands to other kingdoms and conquer them.

Red: And you got an army like that?

Atlan laughed and said

Atlan: We got an army who no one has. Who do you think brought you here.

Red: Who?

Atlan: My Trolls.

Red: Trolls?

Atlan: Yes, magic of Alois has effects on me and I have some powers. Like opening a way to the dark world where all the magical creatures live.

Red almost laughed but then he remembered how Atlan got here.

Atlan: Do you want to join us or not?

Red smiled and said

"Yes"

Atlan smiled back and stood up, he said

"right then, I will be going then"

Atlan and Brett's bodyguard walked out while Brett and Red sat there.

Red: What did he meant when he said trolls got me here?

Brett: Well I kept an eye on your activities since you first worked for my father, I told Atlan that you are going in the Blue Forest and he kept his trolls to keep you in sight. When you were unconscious after beasts attacked you in Blue Forest, They picked you up and got you here.

Red: I was opened up pretty badly, how did i survive that long?

Brett: Atlan told me that Trolls are very intelligent beings, they tend to your wounds and took you through the mountains, curving the Grassy plains to my castle.

Red: Trolls were supposed to be dumb, according to stories.

Brett: Atlan said that it was just a story because of their disfigured faces. Poor things looked dumb.

A servant entered along with both of the bodyguards, holding a new armor and Red's fighting equipment. Red checked the leather armor and looked at Brett because armor was dark red.

Brett: Atlan insisted that we must now wear their colors, I did not wanted to argue and also you don't need to be hiding in shadows so I don't think it will be a problem.

Red picked all the things and walked towards his bedroom. Brett walked towards outside along with bodyguards and servant.

Lord Artis was about to enter his lands, he have been traveling all day with his men. They were on the edge of their lands and they saw some soldiers on the other side. Lord Artis knew that these men must be sent by Brett to receive him. When they reached each other, Lord Artis stopped his horse and said

"How are you captain?"

Captain in front replied

"I am fine sir"

Lord Artis face showed anger and he said

"Where are your manners captain?"

"I remember my manners perfectly and they tell me that I can call you sir, you are no longer a Lord"

Soldiers with Lord Artis came up front and one said

"Watch what you say man"

Captain looked at him and Lord Artis said

"How am I not your lord anymore?"

"Your son is now Lord of these lands and by his ordered you are not welcomed here anymore"

Lord Artis looked at captain in anger and said

"We will see about that"

As soon as his horse took another step, captain drew his sword followed by his men. Lord Artis's men drew their swords too and attacked. Lord Artis had twenty men with him including Renald and him. Captain roughly had fifteen men. Lord Artis got off of his horse and jumped into fighting. After ten minutes Lord Artis and his men were standing with bloody swords among dead bodies of enemy. Then they saw more riders coming towards them and Renald yelled

"Come my lord, our people are against us now"

All men saddled up and horses were running like wind. Riders stopped near the dead bodies. Lord Artis was riding towards one of his friend's lands. One of his childhood friends Lord Clive Jones. Lord Artis could stay there without any problems but as he was at the crossing of roads to Grassy plains and his former lands, he saw Lord Philip and his men going back to their lands. Lord Philip was informed quickly and he came himself at the front to receive Lord Artis.

Lord Philip made a stop and instructed his men to take care of Lord Artis' men. Lord Philip and Lord Artis sat in Lord Philip's tent accompanied with Renald, Ludik. Lord Artis told everything to Lord Philip and Lord Philip offered him to stay at his castle but Lord Artis decided to go as he planned before. After this stop, Lord Artis rode again and at the sundown reached Lord Clive's castle. Lord Clive was very happy to see him. He made arrangements for him and his men to stay. Right now they were sitting at dinner table with Renald and were talking.

Lord Artis: Give me some of your men, I will kill that fool myself.

Lord Clive: Take as many as you want, Brett was the last person I could think of who could betray you.

Lord Artis: He wanted to be a ruler, I guess too much power makes his mind blind.

Lord Clive: I have send some men to see what is happening at your lands but you should rest now, we will see what can we do in the morning.

Lord Artis and Renald went to their rooms and Lord Clive went to his men to give instructions.

At the Brett's castle, he just returned from a hunt and was informed what happened at the border.

Right now he was sitting on the throne and said

Brett: Do not worry, my orders were just to stop him.

Bryte: He will try to return.

Brett: We will be prepared, do not worry.

Bryte: We got another problem.

Brett: What?

Bryte: Your Assassin refuses to obey orders; he says he does not work for you but with you.

Brett: SO what? Let him be man. Anything else?

Bryte: that is all.

Brett: Well I will be going to bed then, I am tired.

Brett went to his bedroom.

The next morning, In the grassy plains Jonald was riding through market along with his men.

He saw Rio walking with his men towards him. Rio saw him and gave him a smile with a nod to the side.

Jonald told his men to carry on and stopped his horse with Rio. Rio said

"Hello Jonald"

"Hello Rio, how are you?"

"Feeling fine"

"Need something?"

"Just wanted to ask something, I think you would know"

"About what?"

"Well rumors are that Red went in the Blue Forest on the command of the throne, is army so weak that they have to use assassins again?"

Rio smiled while Jonald said

"What are you talking about? Red is to be killed at sight plus army can do its job perfectly and right now its job is to keep everybody out of the Blue Forest"

"Well Red went in there for sure, everybody is saying that throne commands it that means Red is working for army"

"Army has nothing to do with this, Red will never return from Blue Forest"

"You sure? He killed Henry in there and returned safely"

Jonald looked at him and said

"Are there any rumors on who paid?"

"Na man, whoever gave the assignment did it very secretly"

Jonald turned his horse and started riding saying

"Well then".

Rio saw him going and walked up to his gang. News of Lord Artis fight reached grassy plains and right now people were talking about it. Everybody has their own theory and all three Generals decided to put the election on hold for a little time

because of the new events because if Brett turned on his own
father that means he could be a threat to the grassy plains and
if people choose a common man then he would not be able to
handle this situation.

14

CHAPTER 14

Lord Artis was at the back door of his castle. He had ten men with him and they all were wearing black leather armors to be stealthy. They traveled silently and secretly to reach his castle at midnight and now there was only one problem which was that there were around ten guards at the backdoor.

This must be Brett being cautious because backdoor never had that many guards. Now Lord Artis had to find a way to get into the castle silently. A straight fight was not a option and it could attract attention. One of the guards started to walk towards the bushes in which they were hiding. Lord Artis signal one his men to take out his dagger but when tat guard came close, he whispered

"Lord Artis, Lord Artis"

Lord Artis got confused and said

"Who are YOU?"

"I was sent by Lord Clive, we have the control of the gate, and he told us where you would be to ease your entrance"

Lord Artis came out and recognized the guard, he was a soldier at Lord Clive's castle. They all walked to the gates and saw the same faces they saw at Lord Clive's castle. They entered the castle silently and now they were twenty in numbers. Lord Artis sent five men to shut the main door and five to kill Brett's bodyguards. He left five to guard the back door and took five with him to his bedroom. Lord Clive told him that Brett is using his bedroom. They walked through hallways to his bedroom and they heard clanking of swords and yelling from the front door.

Somebody woke up or saw the five men sent by Lord Artis. They ran towards the bedroom and two men kicked the door open and entered. Head of one got cut clean off while the other one got stabbed in the heart. Lord Artis saw Brett standing in the room with many soldiers. They started fighting but door was little to any of them to come out or get in without getting killed. Suddenly some soldiers rushed in from the right side of the hallway and Lord Artis started fighting on that side with three of his men supporting him. Lord Clive's men fell back and Lord Artis retreated in the hallway. Now Soldiers came out of the Bedroom too.

They heard footsteps behind and saw some more soldiers, now Lord Artis was surrounded with two men. Brett came out of the bedroom and Lord Artis looked at him with anger and hate. He wanted to kill him and had no mercy in his heart for him. All of a sudden Soldiers on the left side started falling and from behind came the guards who were left to guard the back door. Lord Artis went full retreat and ran towards them. All soldiers followed them.

They threw armors and every decorative thing down to slow the soldiers. As soon they got out, guards threw two oil barrels in the gate and other one threw a torch. Barrels were filled with oil and it caught fire quickly which took in many enemy soldiers running in the front. It was the backup plan guards came up with and it truly saved their lives. Lord Artis and remaining men went running straight into the bushes where Horses were left. They got on the horses and started riding full speed. Clearly someone told Brett of their coming. Lord Artis knew that riders will be sent after them. They kept on riding.

In the morning, Brett was having breakfast and Red entered, Brett said

"Good morning, how was your sleep last night?"

"Not good, people were fighting in the hallways"

"That was an assassination attempt by my father"

"Very good, can I ask you something?"

Red sat on a chair and asked

"What is in the dungeon?"

"what do you mean?"

"I mean i see soldiers taking goats in there your slaughter house in there?"

Brett laughed and said

"There stays my special guests, Atlan sent them "

"Why dungeon?" "You will know when you see them?"

"They eat goats? Raw?"

"Do you remember the missings on the mountains?"

"Yes, that's why I got in this matter"

"Well these guests were the cause of that, and after Jonald saw them and Philip took his men to fight them, Atlan asked me to make them my guest so no one can see them"

"Forest?"

"huh?"

"What about the missings at the forest side?"

"Same, but those are others, these were on the mountains"

"And by those and these, you mean?"

"Ogres"

"Ogres?"

"Ogres"

"How no one ever saw any?"

"I do not know, I did not ask Atlan"

Brett finished his breakfast , he got up and said

"Come with me"

They both walked towards the dungeon, Soldiers were guarding the door, they opened the gate and Both walked in. Torches were lit in the dungeon , Red could see someone in the corner. As they reached Red saw three Ogres. They were double his size in height and in width. They had looked at Brett and Brett said

"Well my friends, Atlan said that tonight you will be traveling back to the mountain and meet him"

Ogres did not say anything, they just grunted and they both walked out. Red said

"I cannot believe all the things happening in my life nowadays"

"Well tomorrow we have our first fight, so be ready"

"Who are we fighting?"

"That we have to decide, we have to begin our invasion now"

Red was standing between a pile of bodies, his armor was covered with blood and his face had drops of dried blood splashed on it. He was standing at the entrance of a small castle accompanied by three soldiers in the same condition as Red. Soldiers were going through bodies and looking for valuables while Red stood there cleaning his sword with a cloth.

Red was commanding a squad of fifty soldiers which was formed by Brett with the announcement that whoever wants to go first in battle can join this squad. From his army a lot of soldiers came but Brett chose these fifty. Brett entered the castle along with his body guards. HIs army has taken over the castle and was currently securing the valley.

Castle was being searched by Red's men and anything valuable was finding its way to the entrance in front of Red. Brett went straight to the throne room to claim this valley. This was a small neighboring valley which was good target to start their invasion. Their Lord was a humble man who always supported Lord Artis with all he could offer.

Brett started the invasion at the hour of dawn and when fighting started Red took his men and stormed the castle. They stood no chance as all the army was fighting because of small numbers they could not protect the castle properly and also fight Brett's army which was three times their size. After a little time, their Lord surrendered and his army laid down their arms.

Brett sent word to Red but they already had finished everybody in the castle and captured Lord's family. At noon Brett was sitting on the throne and his soldiers were standing at the sides of the throne room. They brought Lord and his family in the middle , his family included his wife, a son who was also commander of his army, a daughter whose eyes were red because of crying and two little boys who were scared. Brett spoke.

"Lord Nigel"

Lord Nigel looked at him and said

"What happened to you Brett? why are you doing this?"

" I decided that you are too old to be a Lord now, give young blood a chance old man"

Everybody started laughing, Lord Nigel spoke again

"Laugh all you want, other Lords will bring you to justice"

Brett stopped laughing, he looked at Lord Nigel and spoke.

"They will be standing in front of me too, begging for mercy"

"I am not begging for mercy, what made you think that they will?"

"Because i will set an example out of you"

Brett stopped and looked at Lord Nigel's face which was without expressions. Then He added

"And your family"

Everybody looked at each other, Lord Nigel's face expressions changed a bit. He looked at his son who was standing straight brave. Brett smiled and nodded to Bryte, he came forward but walked past Lord Nigel's sons and grab the wrist of his young daughter. Lord Nigel and his son tried to interfere but soldiers came forward and pulled them back. His wife started crying while holding his young sons. His daughter tried to break Bryte's hold but could not. One of Brett's general spoke in his ear.

"My lord, we should not do anything to women and children, put them in prison or banish them"

Brett replied.

"We need to set an example for the other Lords"

Then he said out loud

"My soldiers, this is a young beauty, untouched. You have fought well and i think you deserve some entertainment"

Soldiers started laughing and Lord Nigel yelled

"Brett let her go"

Brett ignored and spoke to his soldiers again

"you will get her, but first we need to reward one of our fighters who won this castle"

Everybody started chanting Red's name. Lord Nigel face turned scared as he knew the name. Brett spoke again.

"Where is Red Shadow, come forward to claim your reward"

Young women started crying. Red came forward from a corner and started walking towards the center. Soldiers started cheering and chant his name. He stood in front of the young girl and looked in her eyes. She got so scared that she stopped crying. Bryte let her hand go but she could not move. Brett lift his hand and everybody went silent then he spoke.

"Go on Red, she is yours for the day" Red replied and his hard voice echoed in the room.

"She is indeed beautiful, but if you want to set an example you know what you should do?"

"What?" Brett asked.

Red smiled at her, looked at Lord Nigel then back to her. She started sobbing and Red said

"ssshhhhhhhh"

She stopped sobbing, He smiled again and took out his dagger swinging. Her beautiful neck got cut and blood started gushing. Her eyes spread as her hands cover her neck and she fell down. Everybody got shocked. Lord Nigel yelled in pain. Red cleaned his dagger on her dress while her body was shaking.

He turned to Brett and said

"That's how you set an example"

Throne room got silent, only voice was Nigel's wife and kids crying. Red walked out of the room. Brett could not think of anything. Then he broke the silence.

"Take them to prison"

Soldiers who were also shocked slowly began to move and pulled Lord Nigel and his son up. Lord Nigel could not take his eyes off of his daughter who lay there cold. They all walked out of throne room and Brett started distributing the riches and valuables among his army.

All people of Draound came to know what Brett did. Their fear increased when they heard the rumors that Red joined Brett. Some people rejected this news because they did not want to believe it. All the Lords were sending each other letters and trying to figure out what to do. They set their defenses and were waiting for further news. Lord Clive and Lord Artis were sitting in the throne room. Lord Clive just told him what happened and how Brett killed Lord Nigel's daughter. Lord Artis was sad for Lord Nigel. He was a good man and a dear friend of him and to kill his daughter in front of him and his little kids was a terrible thing to do. He spoke.

"i never thought that Brett could do such thing"

"He said he wanted to set an example for other lords, he indeed did"

"What can we do Clive?"

"Lords are talking about launching a counter attack, they are waiting if Brett was just doing it for sport. that way he will stop now and we will not spill our own people's blood"

"Sport? they think this is sport?"

"He just became a Lord, test his army or just making a name for it could be the causes but by his words that setting an example for other Lords does not indicate that"

"Anybody sent any messenger?"

"He killed three Lord's messengers"

Lord Artis sat there quietly. Lord Clive spoke again

"Rumor is Shadow death has joined him, this news is increasing fear in people"

"What? i do not think that an assassin will command an army"

"He works for money, he can do it"

Renald walked in with some letters which were from other Lords. They began discussing them.

15

— ◆ —

CHAPTER 15

B rett was talking to Red and his generals, he was briefing them what to do next but Red was thinking about something else. He remembers a blur vision. Elf standing with her sword but not hitting him and how the sunshine was lighting up her face.. Then he started thinking about the night he heard her saying to max that she lives in the forest.

Red thought that if she lives here that means she is behind the missings. Then he remember the next morning when sun came up and he saw her pointy ears. His hand started rotating his dagger between his fingers. He started to recall the time that he spent with her on her tree but got interrupted by Brett. He was ending the meeting and saying something to him.

"Any questions?"

Red did not hear anything but he said.

"NO"

"So get his kids and wife from the prison and release them with horses"

"Why?"

Everybody looked at him. "I just explained it, we release them, this will take some heat off of us so we can first stable this valley"

Red stood up and walked to prison, he took two soldiers with him. They took both kids out and Red took their mother out. Lord Nigel asked from his cell.

"Where you taking them?"

Red said nothing so a soldier replied.

"They are getting released" Lord Nigel's wife came out, looked Red in his eyes and spoke.

"You will be punished for what you did to my daughter"

Red looked at her and pushed her in front of Lord Nigel's cell along with his kids. He stood behind them.

Lord Nigel spoke

"She is a mother, she is mourning. just let them go"

Red replied

"As a mother she is not mourning enough"

One of the kids came to the bars and held Lord Nigel's hand. Their Oldest son saw Red's eyes and suddenly realized something. He came to the bars and said.

"Don't you touch her, i will kill you"

Red laughed and said

"I will not touch her"

Then he walked up to Lord Nigel holding his kid's hand and said

"Family turns a man into a coward"

He took his sword out and before anyone could understand anything, he drove it through his kid's chest. Their mother sat down while yelling and crying. Lord Nigel started yelling at him. He was still holding his dying son's hand whose body was shaking and spilling blood. Red sheathed his sword and said

"Now she will mourn properly"

He walked back leaving them all. Soldiers took the mother and one remaining son out. gave them horses and released them. Brett was informed of this situation, he did not want to argue with Red but his friend asked him to ask for the reason. Brett came into Red's room. Red was laying in bed. Brett asked him.

"I heard what you did in prison"

"and?"

"a kid?"

"yes"

"May i know the reason?"

"Lords will think twice before going up against you"

"How?"

"That woman would go to other lords or anyone let's say your father who want other lords to go against you would be using her to get sympathy. But now she will not do it, she will remember when she tried to talk back and lost a kid."

Brett could not argue, this would solve some problems for him. Small lords will try to avoid fighting with him. He came back to throne room and started dealing with the matters of the valley.

After a whole day of work, Brett went to bed very tired and quickly went into deep sleep. At midnight, a soldier woke him up, Brett woke up and soldier said.

"My lord, someone broke into prison and took Lord Nigel and his son out."

"What?"

"My lord, it happened just now"

"Then go after them, quick"

Soldier ran out while Brett got out of bed. He wanted to go after them himself but before he could go out. Lord Nigel's son entered with a sword in his hand. He closed the door. Brett was empty handed.

He said to Brett.

"Nowhere to run Brett"

"Address me as my lord"

He jumped on Brett swinging his sword, Brett ducked and punched him on his head. He quickly turned around and strike again. Brett dodged and punched him on his jaw. His jaw broke. Brett said.

"Now you cannot run your foul mouth"

He angrily moved towards Brett and swung his sword again. Brett took a step back and quickly punched him in the neck. Strike was powerful. He could not bear the pain and fainted. Brett took his sword and came out. He ordered some soldiers.

"Pick him up, take him to the ogres. first wake him up then throw him in front of them...."

Next morning, Lord Philip entered Lord Clive's castle with Lord Nigel. Lord Artis came to knew what happened last night. Lord Clive's spies indicated the patrols and location which made Lord Philip to hit an ambush. He told them about Lord Nigel's son that he went to kill Brett. They did not know where his wife went.

No Lord sent any news about her coming to them. It was Lord Clive's guess that she got scared and took her son to somewhere else or in hiding. Near noon they received a news that Brett is still alive meaning that Lord Nigel's last son is dead too. Near evening they received another news that around fifty soldiers marched to an unknown location.

Their commander was unknown. Lord Clive sent letters to every Lord near. But the next morning he came to know that his message was late for a small lord. When his messenger reached his castle. It was in flames. Nobody knew what happened. Army did not even had an chance. Their Lord and his family were killed or burned alive in the castle. Then Brett's army marched on them. They had no choice but to surrender.

Elf was setting up her new tree, she spent last days moving her stuff from old tree to the new one. This tree was near the deep forest. It was dangerous but still she did it, she made it very difficult to see with a lot of branches. Suddenly she heard a blast in the deep forest. She did not know what was that. She waited something to happen but nothing happened.

After some time she again begin moving her stuff. At noon she lied in her tree to take rest. Suddenly she heard thudding, then it grows louder and more. She looked down and saw some ogres walking. They were twice the size of a man and had grey skin. They had big swords and Cleavers. She quickly hides.

She could not understand where they came from all of a sudden. Ogres were holding ropes which were around necks of boggarts. A big creature with a body bigger then a rhino with razor sharp teeth and three horns, one on the nose and two on head parallel to the eyes. They all went past. Elf did not know what to do but she did know that this is not good. After a lot of thinking, She decided to go to Lord Artis to warn him for his innocent people.

At Brett's new castle, Atlan visited. They were sitting in the study room and Atlan was saying

"I have opened the door way, our army has started to pass through"

"Hm, how long will it take?"

"depends on them, they can only pass through if they decide to obey my commands with all their heart and mind"

Brett poured some wine for both of them and spoke

"Why the forest?"

"Doorways have specific opening places, That forest has so much death in it that it nurtures this dark passage naturally"

"What about these trolls? they passed through?"

"Yes, they were my first servants to pass through"

"Now what?"

"Trolls will find them all in the forest, they only are obedient to me but do not know how to find me, they are wandering in the forest so they have to be brought together first"

"well then, how about the King?"

"He will come, with time"

Brett poured some more wine. Atlan spoke again

"Everything is in order here?"

"Yes, we have taken this castle without any bloodshed on our side, i did not even needed your ogres in last two battles"

"Impressive, how did you managed to do that?"

"Well our new friend Shadow death was very helpful, he took his squadron and they ambushed this castle, burned everything"

"Where is the Lord, i would like to ask him some questions"

Brett laughed a little embarrassed.

"Well they were captured in beds. Lord and his family. Soldiers tried to arrest them but Red burned them alive with the castle"

Atlan looked at Brett.

"We need some leverage until our army gathers. we could use them as negotiations if anything happens"

"Red is like that, i can not argue with him. to be honest i was his admirer but now i am scared of him a little"

"We need him, but why so anger?"

"I do not know"

"Give him something as distraction. young man will be happy"

Bryte entered with some food, he placed it on the table. Atlan started eating while Brett took another sip and said

"I gave him the daughter of Lord Nigel"

"Wasn't enough? greedy man"

Brett laughed.

"She was young and beautiful, He killed her in the very spot"

Atlan stopped his hands, Brett said

"Slashed her neck with his own dagger"

Brett added.

"Soldiers are pretty angry about that, she was promised to them after he was done with her"

Bryte said. Brett laughed and said

"We are lucky, i do not think that anyone who got so close to him and still breaths"

Brett and Bryte started laughing but Atlan's voice stopped them

"There is one, still breathing"

Outside the castle, Red was coming back from somewhere. He had an apple in his hand. At the entrance of the castle, army was camping. A soldier wife came to meet him. They were sitting on wine drums and his little daughter was playing on the ground. She looked at Red. His armor was made of leather so he looked unique in all the metal armors.

Red noticed her, her hair were same color as Elf's hair which reminded Red of her. Red showed her the apple. She came running to him and took the apple from his hand. Suddenly her father saw it and thought that she snatched the apple. He came running and return the apple to him and started apologizing

"I am sorry, Sir...My Lord...she is just a kid"

He was so afraid that he forgot what to call him. he picked up his daughter and hugged her.

"She meant no disrespect"

Red took a bite of the apple and started walking. Soldier came quickly to his wife and gave her the daughter.

"Quick go home, do not stop for rest or anything"

His wife noticed his sudden change and asked

"What happened?"

"do not ask questions, move quick and go to your brother's house, not to our house"

She noticed that he was sweating and just packing her stuff. She did as he said and started riding with her daughter.

At night, Elf started her journey towards grassy plains. She was moving very cautiously as she knew that Ogres are in the forest. She heard there roars all day. She came across many half eaten animals. She started moving quickly. At night, whole forest was quite. She walked a long way. She was feeling that someone is watching her but she checked and all she saw was dark forest. It could be her mind playing games.

After sometime she start to hear a little thudding behind her. She started running and the thudding of someone heavy began fast and loud. Thudding was becoming loud so she knew that she can not outrun whoever is chasing her, only way was slip away in darkness. She saw a tree and she quickly hid behind it.

Thudding came close and stopped, then it moved to right and faded away. Elf quickly got out and started walking but after a little time she heard clanking of metal and shouting. This could be humans and she can give them the message. Elf started to run towards the voices and closer she got she realized that there was a fight going on.

She took her sword out and moved quietly. She saw a fire going on around which ogres were fighting with humans. There were two ogres dead and four were still fighting but humans were fighting too good and quick. Ogres stood very little chance. Humans were around thirty and in five minutes they killed two more. One ogre remained.

Ogre hold his cleaver in both hands and roared. He got surrounded by humans. One human attacked him but ogre's cleaver cut him in two from the waist. Before the ogre could recover from his attack, they attacked him and many swords entered his body. Ogre fell and his blood started wetting the ground. Humans started to secure the area. They were talking in an unknown language. Elf sheathed her sword and came in light of fire. All the humans saw her in surprise but one of them said something and they all began to search the area. The one who commanded came forward and said something to her. She spoke.

"I cannot understand"

Man called someone. Another man from the dark comes in to the light. This was a old man. He said to the Elf.

"How did you get pass?"

"What do you mean?"

"May i ask what are you doing here?"

"I live here"

He stopped for a second, and said

"You must be Zagur's daughter.....Theia"

Zagur was her father's name. She said

"Yes, i am"

Old man turned to the young man and told him everything in the language she could not understand. After sometime they were all sitting around fire and she came to know that all these men were elves and the old man knew about his father and mother. These elves crossed over from the a gateway which only opens if someone opens the gateway of a dark world. Elves were called the balance.

Their only purpose was to fight the ogres and balance this world again. Last time this happened when someone opened the door again and again. A lot of elves passed through and they fought alongside humans to defeat them. After winning the battle, they all returned but Theia's father decided to live here. Now again someone has opened the door and dark creatures passed through. Now they had to fight again.

Theia told them about lord Artis who was investigating this mess. But Elves told her that they would fight in the forest first. Finish them with ambushes because it would be very difficult to take them head on. Theia still decided to go to Lord Artis. At dawn, they apart ways and Theia started her journey.

Around noon, she reached grassy plains. Shecovered her ears with the scarf lord Artis gave her. As soon as she walked out,she was confronted by Jonald's men and she was arrested.

16

—— ◆ ——

CHAPTER 16

Lord Artis started gathering an army from all the lords. Every Lord sent as many men as they could spare. Lord Artis was now the commander of the force to help any lord who is under attack. He only had half numbers as Brett's but under his command he could do some serious damage. Lord Clive could not feed another army but every Lord sent food and tents with his men so he did not have any problem hosting all the soldiers. Lord Philip was receiving food from his valley for his army. Lord Artis was sitting with Lord Clive and Lord Philip in Lord Clive's throne room. A servant came and said

"My Lord, some soldiers from grassy plains have arrived, they say they have an important message for Lord Artis"

Lord Artis looked at Renald who was standing beside him. He walked out with the servant. After sometime he walked in with his face showing a lot of happiness. Lord Artis noticed but then he saw soldiers coming in behind him and he understood what was the cause. Theia was walking in between the soldiers. They came in front of the throne and Lord Clive said.

"What message do you bring soldier?"

Soldiers looked at Theia. She came forward and said "I have the message for Lord Artis"

Lord Artis nodded and she started telling all the situation happening in the forest. After getting arrested by Jonald's men, she was brought in front of Jonald and she told him everything. He sent soldiers with her to get her to Lord Artis that if she was not recognized by Lord Artis they were to arrest her and bring her back. At first no one believed her except for Renald and Lord Artis but then she had to remove her scarf which convinced them a little but Lord Clive still did not believe. He said that her ears could be pointy by a disability from birth.

Lord Artis had to take her side and had to tell that she was first captured from Forest by one of his investigating "Officers". Renald signaled her to not to say anything by his eyes. Lord Clive still did not believe it but after Lord Artis believing her completely, he showed a little interest. Lord Philip suggested to contact "Balance" immediately but Theia told them they wanted to ambush them which seemed to them a good idea because soldiers would not go into the forest and now some-one was fighting in the Forest for them. Theia was Lord Artis special guest and was given a room in the castle because if they needed to contact Balance then they would need Theia here. She agreed and Renald was put in charge for looking after her.

At Brett's castle, Red was getting prepared to attack another valley. His men were putting on their armors and Brett was giving them instructions. Red came near them and nodded to soldier. Soldiers started yelling commands to others for moving out and staying low. Brett told Red

"Atlan spoke with me"

"aham?"

"His ogres are getting attacked in the Forest, they will be late to come to our aid"

"Ogres....attacked?"

"Yeah, may be grassy plains army"

"I doubt that, Blue Forest is a very dangerous place and now ogres are also lurking there" "Well, we will see about them but right now you we need our fear to spread. As soon as i attack from front you provide the distraction and General Fisher will handle the rest"

Red nodded and walked towards his men. Whole army was getting ready to march. There plan was to attack the third valley head on. But this Lord was experienced and had a large army. Plan was that Brett will attack and after the attack Red will provide a distraction by attacking their castle but they would be expecting that. So when they take counter measures, their whole strategy will be revealed and then General Fisher who was a general in Brett's army will be doing a third attack from their right side. Providing the surprise element.

At the next dawn, Brett met the enemy Lord at the battle field. After the attack Red attacked the castle and retreated quick because of the large number of soldiers protecting the castle. They were waiting for General Fisher's attack. After a while many riders showed up from right but these were not in the number General Fisher had. They went straight in to the lines of enemies but instead of attacking they took formation with them.

Brett recognized their colors. It was not his army and they were wearing Lord Artis colors. Something went wrong. Brett ordered his army to retreat because he could not took much damage as he wanted to reserve his army and if he tried to take this castle he would receive much damage. His army retreated as their heart burns by the chants of the enemy soldiers. In the retreat, they received Fisher's messenger which told that they were attacked by Lord Artis and took a lot of damage. Brett ordered him to come back to the castle as fast as possible and also to avoid any more fight.

After reaching the castle, he took an overview and estimated that he did not took a lot of damage as Fisher pulled back his forces at reasonable time. Then he found out that Red and his men never made it to castle. This was a problem. Bryte took some men to find out if they were killed. That whole night, Brett stayed awake, strengthening his defenses, he knew his father and his military strategy. He could think that Brett lost a lot of men and could attack this castle. He was also relaxed because he did not took much damage. At next dawn, Bryte came back with Red.

He was unconscious and was wounded badly. Bryte told Brett that by looking at the landscape, he could say that Lord

Artis's riders came from around the castle and attacked Red and his men. Only five or six men survived including Red. Red was quickly took care of and medics were looking after him. This was very bad for Brett. Lord Artis had his own army and his experience in battle was far more than anyone including Lord Philip. After that day, he received a news from his home valley that, Lord Artis riders were spotted and chased but they got away. Brett decided to have a meeting with his Generals.

At Lord Clive castle, Lord Philip was feeling down because Lord Artis single handedly stopped an attack with a lot less men then enemy and Lord Artis was feeling down because Brett got away. But some of his men told that they killed all of the castle raiding party of Brett. They could not confirm who was leading them but it was a good news. Lord Clive's sent some men to recon Lord Artis's home and they told them their defense was tight. They could not get close and got chased. Both sides were now waiting for the next day to see what happens next. Now, Lord Artis was knocking on the door of Theia's room.

He was with Renald who always got nervous around her. Theia opened. She looked very beautiful and stunning in proper dress. Lord Artis could only imagined Renald feelings. HE asked

"Hello Theia, can i have a word?"

Theia nodded and opened her door. They all walked in. Lord Artis sat on the chair and Renald stood beside him while Theia sat on the bed. HE spoke

"How are you?" "I am very good, i heard you won today"

"Well a battle"

"It is a start"

"it is, anything you find inconvenient?"

"Not at all, people are very nice, they get surprised at first when seeing me"

"Well nobody seen an elf here"

Theia smiled a little. Lord Artis spoke again

"i think Renald has explained the situation with me employing Red"

"Yes, he told me that Red was the only guy willing to come in the Forest" "indeed, and you now his profession will make many problems for me here"

"I know but he can not hurt anyone now"

"How do you know?"

"He came back from the deep forest, wounded pretty bad and could not even move"

"You killed him?"

"i was about to, but killing a helpless man did not felt right so i left him there to be eaten by animals"

"He is alive and commanding my Son's army"

Theia's heart pounded.

"Impossible, he could not even open his eyes and no one can get out of the forest in his condition"

Lord Artis stood up

"Well then, i am sorry to hold you in this castle but you are our only source if we have to contact BALANCE"

"Not at all, i am enjoying this life" "IF you need anything just tell Renald"

"I will"

Lord Artis walked out with Renald. They both walked silently then Renald spoke

"She walked around camp yesterday"

"ANd?"

"Soldiers were staring "

Lord Artis stopped his laughter, he said

"Make a list, we will get their eyes plucked out"

Renald understood the sarcasm. He spoke again

"I just meant that..." "Come on Renald, don't be such a baby. She can do whatever she wants. She is my guest and has done a great job providing the information she provided and as for the soldiers, they have never seen such a beauty. You want her then talk to her"

Renald remained silent .

17

CHAPTER 17

Five days have passed, Red was still in bed. He took pretty bad wounds but he was getting medical attention from one of Atlan's troll. When Red opened his eyes, he saw the troll for the first time. Troll had a disfigured face and had Brown skin which looked like dirt and had hair looking like grass.

Red understood how they were able to move in Blue Forest unnoticed. This troll never spoke anything but according to Brett he was treating Red with medicine made with human ingredients and magic mixed up with them. Red could feel his recovery at a miraculous rate. He suffered very bad hit on head when Lord Artis's riders came from back.

Red and his men were caught off guard. Red killed one of them but a rider rode him over with his horse. Horse hoof opened up his head. But now Troll was treating him and in five days Red was almost able to walk without feeling shooting pains in his head.He was briefed with the situation. Small rider groups were often spotted and chased. Lord Artis was looking for a opportunity. Red was sitting in castle's garden. He had an apple in his hand. He was looking in the sky. Red heard a faint scream from inside the castle. It was a girl's voice. Right then a servant came to Red and said

"Lord Brett sent a message, he asked you to come to your room"

Red stood up and walked to his room. It took some time because he could not walk with his regular speed. No one was allowed in this part of the castle because of Troll attending to Red. When Red reached his room, he saw Atlan and Brett leaving his room along with three trolls. Atlan saw Red and smiled. He said

"I bring you a gift Red"

Brett's face showed a little anger, he said

"It was meant for one of our very important man so you better not waste it"

All walked past Red while he stood still. After getting at a distance where Red could not hear them. Brett said in low voice "It might make a problem"

Atlan smiled and replied

"We need to control him, we need something and this will give us the answer"

"Whatever you say"

Brett replied and they kept on walking.

Red waited for them to go. Then he opened the door. There was a girl tied up on his bed with his face covered with a sack. Her pitch black long hairs told Red that it was the Elf. He exhaled a big breath. Elf heard it and said

"Who is there?"

Red did not reply. She asked again

"Who is there? Release me"

Red's hand went up to her face to remove the sack but he stopped. His heart started pounding and he felt a little nervous. he thought to himself

"What the hell Red"

Elf screamed again

"Get this off of my head"

He shook his head from left to right.

He walked out of the room, this was very bad for him. He always was brave and a symbol of terror for his enemies because he had no weaknesses. Nobody knew who he was or anyone who could be used to get Red emotionally hurt or blackmailed. This was his secret. Red walked towards Brett's study where Atlan had his meetings with Brett. Bryte saw him coming, he opened the door for him and both walked in. Atlan was sitting with Brett. They both saw Red and Brett said

"there goes the Elf, Bryte send someone to clean his room"

Atlan said

"Why you killed her Red, Brett was giving it to one of his own man as a reward but i insisted to give her to you and such beauty"

Red sat on a chair and said

"She is alive, just remove her from my room, i do not need anything "

Bryte walked out of the room. Brett said

Brett: We just thought it will provide you some entertainment.

Red: Do not need any entertainment. I was promised land and wealth.

Atlan: You will get it, do not worry. Some problems are delaying it.

Brett: I told you about elves right?

Atlan: I did not know about them, they crossed too and now ambushing our ogres in the forest. My trolls are busy finding them but elves found some of them too.

Red: Anything else which could pass through?

Atlan: i do not know.

Brett: Does not matter, we have started it now so cannot stop.

Red nodded and troll walked in. That meant that he was looking for Red to give medication. After medication Red go to deep sleeps. Red walked out with him. Brett said to Atlan

"How we will control him now?"

"He wants wealth and lands, we already controlling him, what you will do with Elf?"

"Put her in prison, will give her to the my man"

They both kept on talking.

At Lord Clive's castle. Renald was sitting with all the Lords. He was injured badly and was telling the story. Theia went on walks everyday and this time she rode with Renald to the nearby Forest. This was another little forest. In the Forest, someone attacked them which Renald could not see. Someone attacked him from behind and when he woke up. Theia was gone. Lord Philip sent Ludik to look into the Forest. She was their way to contact Balance. Lord Clive instructed his soldiers to investigate Locals. Renald asked to investigate the army too. Which Lord Artis declined because it would make soldiers think that their Lords do not trust them. At night, all Lords were having dinner in the dining room. Lord Clive said

"An Elf has been seen in Brett's castle"

Lord Philip: Theia?

Lord Clive: My men do not know.

Lord Artis: What is the Elf doing there?

Lord Clive: She is in prison.

Lord Philip: Well it could be Theia, Ludik did not find anything in the forest yet.

Lord Artis: How Brett's men came this far without being seen?

Lord Clive: Traitors may be, i got my men there so it is possible that have his men here too.

Lord Artis: What we will do about it?

Lord Clive: We are doing all we can, trying to investigate silently.

Night passed, it was before dawn . Sky was showing the first lights of the day. Jonald was washing his face with water. His family was still sleeping. He had a younger sister and a father. His father used to be a soldier in army. His mother passed away many years ago. Jonald joined the army when he was sixteen and got promotions due to his excellent work and performance. Last promotion was from captain to General which was not possible in normal circumstances.

Jonald put his armor on the bed. Metal clanked a little loudly and he stopped. His family was sleeping and he did not want to wake them up. He stood there for a second listening if someone woke up but his ears only heard the morning calls of birds. His face showed a little relief. He placed his sword on the bed too. He was about to put on his armor but there was loud knock on the main door. He walked to the door and opened. There was a soldier standing with a horse. Jonald asked

"Soldier?"

Before soldier could answer, a fireball fell behind the soldier in the street with a little blast. Jonald almost jumped. Soldier turned to the fireball and then turned back to Jonald

"Well General"

Jonald quickly came out and took the reins of the horse from him. He got up the horse and said to soldier

"Bring my horse, my armor and sword to barracks"

Soldier nodded and Jonald rode off. Jonald turned his horse towards the castle besides where barracks were built. Streets were empty at this time of the morning. Jonald heard some more light blasts and saw the smoke lines on the sky. He reached barracks and saw soldiers getting ready to fight. Barracks were full meaning every soldier was called from the houses. Soldier were shouting orders to move to the plains towards Miller pass. Jonald asked a soldier.

"What is happening soldier?"

"An army came out of nowhere, Miller pass look outs did not send any news"

Jonald turned his horse towards Miller Pass, As soon as his horse crossed the houses, he could see a vast number of men near the mountains. They had flags up and trebuchets which were throwing fireballs in the city. Jonald came close to his army which was starting to form up. He stopped his horse near the General's tent and walked in. Both Generals were present and were discussing the situation. They saw Jonald and Jonald asked

Jonald: What is happening?

Salvador: We are being attacked, we do not know how they got passed the Miller pass lookouts but they are here.

Jonald: Sun is not up yet and already I can tell that they are four times are size.

Riendo: We know that Jonald but right now we need to focus. We need a strategy to beat this army or at least hold them off till help comes from other lords.

Soldier walked in with Jonald's armor and sword. Jonald started wearing armor.

Salvador: We will not attack first. Citizens are being ordered to evacuate right now towards the opposite side. We need as much time as possible.

Jonald: Any idea whose army is this?

Riendo: No, flags are new.

Jonald: Brett?

Salvador: not possible, He does not have a army that big.

Jonald wore his sword and said

Jonald: How are they throwing fireballs?

Riendo: Right now, in this light and distance we can only see some structures rotating and fireballs just fly and go above our heads to the city making an arc.

Salvador: They are attacking the city without even getting in the city.

A soldier ran in giving them the news that enemy is marching forward. All three generals came out and saw that enemy soldiers were moving forward. Salvador yelled.

"We do not attack, we hold the attack and buy time"

Orders were yelled through whole army. Jonald are Riendo were going through ranks and inspecting. Day light was getting more and more but sun was still down behind the mountains. Enemy army marched closer and closer. Generals saw that there was no proper march in them, they were walking normally.

When they came close Soldiers saw that they had some big entities with them. They were twice the size of a normal person and width was also twice. Faces could not be seen in this light. These big enemies could be seen among the army because of their long heights and they were also many in numbers. Enemy came closer and closer. Now they could hear their voices and shouts. Language could not be understood. They were talking in an unknown language. They crossed the standard line of attack and came more close. Riendo signaled and soldiers took out their swords. Salvador said

"Are they going to attack us while walking? Rush line is supposed to be one chalk"

After coming more close, they stopped and now the distance between both armies were half a chalk. They could easily see each other and if they rushed each other, it would take only thirty seconds to reach. Big entities were not in the front lines and normal soldiers could be seen holding weapons. They were chanting and shouting. Then they all went quite and a man came in forward. He turned around and shouted something. Enemy soldiers started running towards the army. Jonald said to Salvador

"Well we got ourselves a fight General"

General Salvador turned his horse and started yelling

"Hold the lines, no breaking and no running. Enemy have no discipline of even marching properly. They cannot fight you"

Soldiers took the holding stances. Their hands griped their swords tightly and shields were brought forward. Riendo ordered archers to knock the arrows. Archers obeyed the order.

Riendo ordered to fire. Arrows went flying towards the enemy and brought down many of the running.

Riendo realized that enemy was too close to give traditional orders. He ordered archers to fire at will. Enemy soldiers came close and front line shields locked their feet into the ground. First impact happened. Enemy slammed into the shields. Shields absorbed the impact and started stabbing the enemy from sides. enemy had swords and leather shields. They started swinging their swords. Swords started clanking and blood started splashing. Salvador and Riendo were yelling orders. Soldiers held off the first wave with ease. Clearly enemy lacked discipline of proper fighting. Enemy went back after the first wave. Archers took down some more retreating enemies. Salvador spoke loudly

"These idiots do not know how to fight"

Soldiers started chanting. Enemy was regrouping for second wave. Second charge began and Jonald yelled

"Get ready for the second wave"

Enemy soldiers were coming running. Soldiers got ready for the second wave but Sun came up from behind the enemy. Soldiers were now having difficulty to see the enemy. Sunlight was blocking their vision. Suddenly arrows came from above and many soldiers got hit. Enemy took the advantage of the sun and hit them blind. Soldiers could not see the arrows coming and did not take any protection. Front line was the aim of the enemy and now it was broken from many places. Riendo yelled

"Form the front line, do not let any one through"

But enemy was too close, They ran through the front line and started cutting soldiers. Full on fight broke out. Enemy was not trained for the formal combat but they did know how to fight. Both sides started losing men quickly. Riendo and Jonald jumped into combat and started fighting. In the mean time, Salvador formed up the front line again and soldiers held off the coming enemy. Enemy tried breaking in again but they did not succeeded. After a little fight, they started retreating. Salvador looked at his army. They did not take much damage. Some soldiers were killed and others took wounds. Jonald rode to Salvador and said

"There is another army approaching from right."

Salvador looked to right where Blue forest was and saw same flags as enemy's. This army was also in same numbers as the front enemy. They could not take these numbers from two sides. Riendo came close and said

"Enemy is coming for the Final wave"

Final wave meant that all enemies are going to rush. Salvador looked in front and saw the enemies approaching. From behind them, small fireballs rose and came straight into army ranks. Many soldiers got hit. These fireballs were low, fast and many in numbers. This was a new problem. Ranks got distributed and soldiers started forming them up again. More fireballs came and enemy impacted the front line. Everybody started fighting. Archers were firing arrows. Swords were cutting flesh off of bodies. Jonald said to Salvador

"We have to retreat, Enemy from the right is close now. We will be butchered"

Salvador looked around for a second and yelled

"Retreat, Fall back"

Everybody started retreating. Jonald was riding his horse and fighting. He was giving orders to retreat to soldiers. Enemy saw this retreat and they started to attack more quickly. They retreated to the houses. Salvador ordered them to fall back to opposite side and follow the civilians. Fighting was still going on and now they were fighting in the streets. Houses were getting burned by enemy soldiers. Jonald was fighting on his horse.

He did not know where other Generals went. They all jumped into combat and were separated. Jonald was fighting in the market. He killed an enemy but could not see the other one who cut of his horse's neck. Jonald fell down but quickly got up. He held his sword with both hands and attacked the enemy. Enemy dodged the attack and did a counter attack. Jonald leaned back and pushed his sword into his chest. Enemy soldier got pierced and fell down. Two soldiers came to Jonald's aid. No one other was around but they could hear fighting going on. Smoke was starting to fill the town. One of the soldiers spoke

"Civilians are out of the city, they are moving to Lord Clive's land"

Jonald said

"We have to get out too, Enemy is far greater in numbers then us"

All of a sudden they heard a loud growl. It was like an animal growl. From a street, an ogre came in front of them. They all got shocked. They only heard about ogres in legends and now one was in front of them. Ogre saw them and started running towards them with his cleaver. Jonald and both soldiers started running opposite of him.

They had no idea what to do. They turned into a street but they saw another ogre fighting with some soldiers. They stopped running. Chasing ogre reached them. One of the soldier held his sword up and took fighting stance. By looking at him Jonald and the second soldier did the same. First soldier yelled loudly and started running towards the ogre. Both followed him. Before they could reach them.

A sword hit ogre from the back and his neck got half cut from behind. From behind the ogre, Rio came and started striking ogre's neck again and again. Ogre fell down. General Riendo was with him. General was without his horse. He looked behind them and saw other ogre still fighting. He ran past them and joined the fight. Jonald and soldiers looked at each other. Jonald lifted his shoulders up and ran to Riendo's aid. After two minutes, they took down the ogre. Riendo was out of breath. He said

"Second enemy army entered the city, they have many ogres and some rhino kind of animals"

One of the soldier said

"What are the orders General?"

Riendo spoke again

"Leave the city, we cannot hold it any longer, We have no choice. We are going to Lord Clive's lands. There we will re-group and plan an attack"

They all started to run towards outer houses. They had to fight some more enemies but they managed to get out of the city. All soldiers were ordered to go to Lord Clive, they were told not to stop for regrouping. Jonald looked back at the city where smoke was rising from different places. He could see the soldiers coming out in small numbers. Riendo said

"Do not worry Jonald, we have only lost the battle. War is yet to come"

18

CHAPTER 18

At lord Clive's castle, everyone knew about what happened at Henry's valley. Henry's soldiers were coming in small groups. Civilians reached before them. Lord Clive and other lords were on their toes trying to take care of them. General Salvador did not reached while Riendo and Jonald reached Lord Clive's castle at night.

Nobody had any idea what happened. News were spreading about ogres and some soldiers were saying that it is false because Henry's army was trying to justify their running. But everybody saw the elf and it was hard not to believe. New tents could be seen in great numbers.

Lords of Dround were sending letters to each other. Brett was one problem but now a foreigner army was in the land. Only half of Henry's army survived. Second enemy army entered the city from the right and flanked the soldiers. Ogres, trolls, big three horned rhinos and men.

They destroyed houses, killed men and destroyed anything which stood in the way. Fireballs and arrows took many lives. Many wounded soldier stayed behind to fight because they were afraid that they will only slow their comrades down. They preferred to fight and die with honor. Soldiers were sad and angry because of the loss of their brothers in arms. In the Castle, dinner table was set. Lord Clive, Lord Artis, Lord Nigel, Lord Philip, Renald, General Riendo and General Jonald were sitting. They all were eating and discussing the situation.

Artis: We need a plan.

Nigel: The numbers you are telling General, it would not be possible.

Clive: But also they cannot fight against proper forms.

Riendo: We saw them fought, they can't fight the forms but they can fight once they are through.

Philip: And now they got three horned rhinos with them. They can break the ranks easily.

Jonald: Also, they can just attack us from far with fireballs.

A servant came in with a letter and handed it to Lord Clive. Lord Clive opened the letter and read it. Then he said.

"Brett is having a big feast and a big part of foreigners just joined him in the feast"

Everybody went silent. This meant that Brett formed an alliance with the foreigners. This was bad.

Artis: I will break his neck myself. i do not care if war is won or not, i want that fool's head.

Philip: We cannot be thinking about revenge or an individual. We have to survive this.

Clive: Can we kill their beasts?

Jonald: A paid killer killed one ogre alone, then we took down one more. it is hard but possible. Beasts are also living things.

Riendo: We were fighting in the market, a rhino just came through tearing a house down. My horse got pierced with its horn. I got separated from my men. I found that man in the street with bags of gold. He was trying to save his gold rather than his life. Had to talk sense into him to leave the gold and leave the city. I did not know that he was a paid killer.

Jonald: You must have heard his name, Rio. He is a killer for hiring. Today he took down an ogre alone.

Philip: But we lost too many men today.

Nigel: Then what do you suggest Philip?

Philip: I hate to say this and this is not a warrior's way but we need to plan assassinations. Brett head and whoever is controlling foreigners.

Clive: This could be a solution but people who come to other lands will not go back just because their king is gone.

Artis: But it will make them a little weak.

Riendo: Who is controlling ogres?

Clive: You said that they are fighting with them, probably same king or the alliance. we will see.

Clive wrote something on a paper and gave it to a servant. Servant went out.

Clive: This means that we are exposing our spies there. They won't be able to stay there after this.

Jonald: Greater good will be achieved.

Clive nodded. Ludik entered the room with General Salvador following him. General Salvador looks gave away that he had a long journey. He had mud, blood and sword cut all over his armor. Ludik said

"General is here my lords"

Salvador walked to an empty chair and sat. He picked up a glass and started drinking water.

Philip: We thought you got killed General.

Salvador: They tried but i got away.

Artis: What happened?

Salvador: After their second army got in the city, i ordered everyone to evacuate. me and some of the soldiers stayed behind to get every one out but their rhinos came in. we hid in a house, and when got the chance. We moved swiftly and silently.

Nigel: Any idea? who these people are?

Salvador: No my lord, language was new, and skin was pale. Miller lookouts did not say anything. They have ogres with them. I think history is repeating itself.

Clive: What do you mean General?

Salvador: All the legends we use to hear from our mothers to put us to sleep. Draound great war. Legends told us the same pale skin enemies with ogres with them. If we had elves, it would be same.

Artis: We had an elf.

Salvador: What do you mean?

Artis: An elf was with us but Brett kidnapped her.

Salvador smiled a little but saw that every one was serious. He said

Salvador: Actual elf?

Philip: Yes, she told us that Blue forest was some kind of opening passage for these ogres, more elves passed and they are currently fighting in forest.

Salvador: Well, how many? can they help us fight?

Clive: Around thirty which are not enough.

Salvador: i found out that they also have wooden structures, have some bow and arrow mechanism. They used it throw fireballs at us. I saw them moving two kinds. One was big and i think that's what they used to throw fireballs in the city and second were small which i figured was used on our army.

Jonald: So what should we do my lords?

Artis: We move civilians to farther valleys. Ask lords to send men. We cannot let these foreigners take control.

All lords agreed on this. They finished eating and everyone went to their rooms. At midnight, Lord Artis heard a knock on his door. He opened and saw Jonald. Jonald slapped him on his face. His face hurt a lot. Jonald's face was red with anger. Artis knew what this was about. Jonald said in anger

"Once this is all over, you will pay for your crimes"

Artis knew that if Jonald arrested Theia and delivered her to him, Theia must have told him the whole story. Rest was easy for Jonald to figure out. Jonald walked away and Artis closed his door. He came back to his bed and sat on it. He knew it will not be good for him.

At Brett's castle, feast was going on. They were joined by King Adlard himself. Brett and Adlard were sitting side by side and their soldiers were eating food and enjoying. Atlan was the one who was translating between Brett and Adlard. Adlard was a man with height. He had little eyes with black hairs. He had a squeaky voice. Today their army crossed the wastelands and through the mountains, they entered grassy plains. They took over grassy plains with ease. Because of their second army which came from the Blue forest. A servant came to Brett with a letter. He read it and told Atlan something. Atlan told it to Adlard and Adlard started laughing. After the feast, Everybody left except Brett and his two bodyguards, Atlan, Adlard and Red. Atlan said

"King would like to see the prisoner now"

Everybody stood up. Brett nodded to Red to join them. They all walked to the prison. Red knew that they are going to see the Elf. He walked slowly. Guards opened the door. Prison was empty as all prisoners were fed to the ogres. Only one cell had someone in it. They all walked in front of it. Elf was sleeping. Brett said

"Wake her up"

Red's heart started pounding a little. He moved behind Brett. Bryte went close and beat the cell bars with his sword. Elf woke up and looked here and there. Adlard started laughing. Elf saw them and said nothing.

Adlard started speaking and Atlan translating

"Your people defeated us once with humans. But now look at you, you are in prison. I did what you did years ago, i joined the humans this time and now they are helping me to take over this land. This time, it does not matter how many of you pass through. I will kill you and everyone who stand in my way".

Adlard took out his throwing knife. Red's hand moved to his knife automatically. Elf's eyes showed fear. Adlard laughed and said

"Look in her eyes, she is scared already. I won't kill you because of Brett. He have something else planned for you"

Adlard put back his knife and walked towards prison gate. Everyone followed. Red stood there and looked at his hand which was still on his knife. Red did not know what he felt. Why his hand was on the knife. What would he do if Adlard killed the Elf. Everyone left. Prison gate closed with a loud noise. Elf saw Red standing there. Her eyes showed hatred and sadness. She felt her heart beating fast in her chest. Red was wearing their colors. Elf's tears gathered up in her eyes. She spoke for the first time.

"You survived"

"Disappointed?" Red's hard voice echoed in the empty prison.

"I should have killed you"

Her voice broke down while saying the last sentence. Red noticed it and took a look at her. She was wearing a brown dress. It was tore from places. Her hair were spread. light from the torch was lighting her face. She had a tired look on her face and her beautiful eyes were full of tears.. Red could not look into her eyes. He looked away.

"can't face me?" she asked.

Red said nothing.

"You broke my trust so many times Red"

"It was your mistake to trust me"

"Yes it was, it is clear now, but why can't you face me"

Red said nothing.

She got up and came close to the bars.

"What happened ? you were supposed to be a ruthless killer. Now you can't even face a girl?"

Red tried to lift his face up but could not

" Go away Red, I have no respect for you"

Red stood there with his face down. She yelled

"Go away, you are just a mindless soul, you have no sympathy for anyone"

Red started walking. She yelled again

"You are evil, you are filth, You will die in filth"

Red came to the door and Guards opened the door from outside.

"You will die alone, No one will bury you and no one..."

Door closed behind Red and Elf's voice stopped. Red walked towards his room but her voice was echoing in his head. His heart became heavy but he kept walking. Red came to his room and saw the troll sleeping in a corner. He slapped the wine glasses off of the table. Glasses hit the ground and shattered. Troll did not woke up and kept on sleeping. Elf's voice kept screaming at him in his head. He could not forget her words. He sat on the bed with his head in his hands. A letter was on his bed. He opened it and saw the reading. It was from Brett.

"Tonight, do not sleep. We are expecting some guests"

Red sat against bed crown and kept thinking about the elf. Her eyes were full of tears. His heart became more heavy. He said to himself

"I need to kill somebody"

Then he saw the letter lying on his bed. He put his head back and closed his eyes. He started humming the tune he hums.

At mid night, Door opened silently. A shadow walked in. He put his steps very carefully. He came close to the bed. He raised a knife above his head but before he could stab Red. Red said

"I will keep it honest with you chief, there is a troll behind you"

Shadow quickly turned around and his head came in between two big hands of the troll. Red quickly got up and cut shadow's throat. Small voices started coming from his cut neck. Troll started drinking the fresh warm blood spilling from his neck. Red put the knife on the table and walked out. He made his way through silent hallways to Brett's room. Someone was standing in front of his room and about to walk in. Red yelled

"Why you so slow? just walk in"

Assassin turned to Red and door opened itself from inside. Brett was standing there with his sword in his hand. Assassin took a swing but Brett dogged it. Red came close in the mean time and kicked Assassin's chest. He fell to the ground. Brett walked out but the Assassin took another swing which cut Brett's knee. Brett jumped up but coming down he pointed the sword at Assassin. Sword went straight into his gut. Assassin yelled. Brett quickly gutted him from chest to navel.

"I was prepared for him, now i got a cut on my knee"

Red just lifted his shoulders up. They both then walked to Adlard's room but found another Assassin dead. Adlard was sitting on his bed with a bloody knife. He nodded because Atlan was not present. Brett and Red walked back. Before going in his bedroom Brett said

"Stay awake, just to be safe, i don't know how many spies my father got here."

Red came to his room where troll was eating the body. He lied on bed and closed his eyes.

Next morning, Lord Clive told everyone that Assassinations failed.

Artis: Someone close to you is telling Brett everything, when I ambushed the castle, Brett was prepared that night too.

Clive: These type of orders are sent by my most trusted servants. Now half of my spies are dead.

Philip: We should focus on army exercises. We have soldiers of many lords and they have no co ordination with each other.

Nigel: Philip is right. We need spies there and cannot waste more on Assassinations attempt.

Ludik: My lords, it is not my place to say but whatever we do, Brett will know. We need to get spies from our camp.

Jonald: Anyone got any suspects?

Nobody said anything.

Clive: Well from now on, with all due respect. No one will be allowed in the meetings. No managers, no bodyguards, no right hands. All letters will be sent by my hand and if you have to send a letter bring it to me.

Everybody nodded. Ludik, Renald, Riendo and Jonald stood up and walked out. All the bodyguards moved out too. Lord Clive wrote this order on a paper and gave it to a servant. Then he told all the servants to go out. After everybody moved out. They started discussing the situation. Five minutes later, a servant walked in with a letter. Lord Clive read it and asked for a pen. After signing it he was about to give it to the servant but then he stopped and asked Lord Artis.

"Renald have a cousin in Lord Nigel's valley?"

"Yes, why?"

"He wrote a letter and told his cousin that he won't be able to make it to his wedding"

"Well, he is unmarried but he is not of marriage age yet, he is eleven years old"

Lord Clive asked the servant.

"Renald gave it to you?"

"No my Lord, he was at messenger's chamber when I reached with your order. So messenger gave it to me instead of sending it"

Lord Clive looked at Lord Artis. Lord Philip said

"Call him here, we need to confirm this before sending"

Servant walked out. After sometime he came back and said

"My lords, Renald is not in his room. His baggage is nowhere to be found and his horse is not in the stable"

Lord Clive sighed. Lord Philip asked Lord Artis

"How many traitors are in your employees?"

Nigel: Watch your tongue Philip.

Philip: I am just stating facts here Lord Nigel, I meant no disrespect but his son betrayed him and his manager was spying on us all along.

Artis: I did not know, I did not even suspected him.

Clive: That means he gave elf away too.

Artis: He liked that girl very much. He secured her for himself. I am sure Brett is keeping her alive for him.

Philip: Well at least we got the spy out.

Lord Clive smiled. Lord Artis started laughing. General Salvador walked in.

Nigel: General Salvador, you will be representing grassy plains in these meetings.

Salvador: I will, I just heard the new orders.

Philip: And we got the results too.

Then Lord Philip started to tell him the whole story.

That noon, army exercises started in Lord Clive's Valley. Soldiers started practicing their fighting and co ordination. Different Battalions were made to carry out different tasks. Main problem was the fireballs and how to avoid them. Everybody was presenting their ideas. Long bows were ordered so they can fire to long distances. For ogres, Steel head arrows were ordered dipped in poison.

Soldiers were practicing to take down bigger enemies. It was officially announced that foreigners have an alliance with Brett and also Red shadow was one of the commanders for Brett's army. This spread fear into the army but Generals and Lords gave speeches to the soldiers on how one traitor made an alliances and threatens to take over their land. Lord Nigel told everybody in his speech about when Brett gave his daughter to Red Shadow and he killed her in front of his eyes.

Lord Artis told everyone that even though Brett is his son but he will give big reward to the person who bring him his head and even bigger if they capture him alive and bring him to Lord Artis so he can kill Brett himself. Their speeches brought confidence and bravery to the soldiers. Soldiers started their exercises with a new spirit. Generals ordered captains and lower ranks officers to tell soldiers the stories of history and specially stories of Draound war, to keep soldiers blood warm. History was repeating itself and this time it was up to every man to die nameless or mark their name in legends for coming generations to remember. If they fail this time, there won't be their generations to live in these plains.

At night, at Brett's castle, dinner was served. Everybody was present. Brett and Adlard were laughing and enjoying their food. Red was sitting on a corner table alone. Brett stood up and everybody quite down. Brett spoke

"I just got news of a very special person, he served us well and because of him I have survived two assassinations. One of which was carried out by my father himself. Tonight that person is here with us"

Everybody chanted. Brett smiled and then spoke again

"Gentleman, please welcome one of my dearest friends. Renald"

Everybody looked at the door. Renald walked in and everybody started chanting his name. Renald face showed that he just arrived at the castle. He was riding whole day because he was afraid that Clive would send soldiers after him. Renald walked till he was in front of Brett and Adlard. He bowed. Atlan started telling Adlard about who Renald was and what has he done for Brett. Renald spoke

"My lord, I was loyal to you and did all I could to serve you. But this morning, Lord Clive gave an order and before I could send the letter, it got caught. I had to get out or I would have lost my life. I am truly in regret that I could not serve you more."

Brett laughed and said

"Renald, do not worry my friend. You have served enough and now Adlard's army is here. We do not need spies anymore. We will crush their armies and take these lands and more lands far beyond."

Everybody started chanting. Renald looked around with a smile. He bowed to everyone and soldiers started laughing. Brett said

"Sit here with me Renald, you are one of my good friends, I have known you from my childhood and you saved my life two times. I have arranged a gift for you."

Renald knew what was his gift. After all he was the one to give it to Brett first. He walked up to Brett and sat beside him. Brett said to a servant

"Bring in the gift"

Servant went out the door and everybody started to enjoy the feast. Brett started introducing Renald to King Adlard. But Renald was not even listening. His eyes were at the door. He could not wait to see Theia.

Door opened and Theia entered through. She was surrounded by four guards. She had a golden dress on with her hair properly combed. Brett sent some female servants to prepare her for this event. Renald was surprised a little that she is walking without being in any chains. But then he saw the guards behind her. They had their swords out and pointed at her back. If she stopped, swords would give her a cut. They walked till they reached in front of Brett. Everybody was stunned by how beautiful she was. Renald never saw her in a golden dress and he forgot to even blink. Red was still eating his food, he knew who was the gift. Brett said

"This is our special guest, she is an elf and in exchange of Renald's services. From now she is given to Renald"

Red's hands did not stop. He knew that this was the plan but he felt like someone grabbed his heart. Everybody started making cheerful noises. A big smile took over Renald's face. Theia lifted her face up and saw Renald. Renald did a little nod. Renald spoke to Brett

"I would like to make her my lawful wife"

Adlard said something, Atlan spoke

"King says, What a gentleman"

Everybody started laughing. Theia looked around and saw Red. Red was eating and drinking wine. Theia spoke for the first time.

"I would die before becoming a wife to you humans"

Brett spoke

"She is a fighter, Can u handle her Renald?"

laughs emerged in the room. And someone yelled

"Renald I can help you with that if you want"

Soldiers started laughing again. Another one said

"I can too, I have six kids and would not hurt to have another"

Soldiers started beating their mugs on the tables. Theia felt disrespected. She was nothing but meat to them which they could taste whenever they wanted. She looked at Red again. He was pouring some more wine. Adlard spoke and Atlan said

"King says, You all are being very disrespectful to a woman"

Everybody went silent. Then Adlard added and Atlan spoke with a smile

"But since we are here, I want to join too because girls like these do not come around everyday"

Soldiers started laughing and beating their mugs on the table. Brett and Renald laughed. Brett whispered to Renald

"You got yourself a gem Renald, everybody wants a piece of her"

Renald spoke

"I know my lord, but situation can get a little messy if she stays. remove her from here"

Brett nodded and said out loud

"I know she is beautiful my lads, but Renald chose her as his wife so hold your horses"

Soldiers collectively said

"aaahhhhhhh shit"

Brett laughed and said

"Get her to Renald's room, He will make her his wife tonight, We will see about lawful procedures tomorrow"

Red stood up, lifted his wine glass up and said

"To Renald and his new wife"

Soldiers lifted their mugs up and drank. Everybody was surprised that Red cheered for someone. Guards took Theia to Renald's room. After the feast, Renald came to Red's table who was quite drunk. He had wine glasses piled up in front of him. Renald said

"You should be easy on the wine Red, You are drunk"

"We are not going to war, we are just sitting here. I killed more people than this war in my normal life"

"Well, I came to thank you for the toast. It is an honor to be toasted by you"

Red smiled and said

"Do not worry, you are comrade"

Renald saw that Red was under wine. He asked Brett to send him to his room. Brett ordered two guards and they took Red on their shoulders. Then Brett sent Renald to his room too. Renald came to his room but before entering. He gave a pet down to his cloths and set his hair. He entered and saw Theia chained to the bed. He sat on the bed. Theia looked at him with hate. He said

"It is a new life Theia"

"For you Renald"

"I am giving you respect, honor and my name"

"I do not need anything from you"

Renald sighed

"Why don't you understand? I love you"

"Ask me if I care"

"You will be my wife, I have no intentions of even touching you against your will"

"But you want to marry me against my will"

"Some things we have to do to get our love"

Theia said nothing.

"Give me a chance Theia, I will prove that I am good for you"

"I just want to go back to my old life, You know you are killing innocent people"

"I am not the killer, invasions happen, I just chose the winning side"

"I do not care, give me my freedom"

Renald laughed a little.

"What if I don't?"

"Then a friend can help her to get her freedom"

A voice came into the room. Renald jumped off the bed and stood up. He looked around and saw all torches were out except one. He did not noticed it. He said

"Red?"

"Naaaaaa, green"

Voice was coming from a dark corner.

19

CHAPTER 19

Red was hung over, he woke up at noon. Troll was not in the room. Red stood up and walked out. He took a bath. He came to dining room and asked for breakfast. Then he asked for wine. He sat there drinking for two hours. He threw up a couple of times. Servants cleaned up. All of a sudden Brett entered with his two body guards. Red looked at him. Looked like they were riding. Brett was angry. He came in and kicked a chair. Bryte yelled

"Bring wine"

Servants quickly sat up the table. Brett was sitting in anger. Red poured wine for him. Brett drank the whole glass in one gulp. Red poured up again. Brett did it again. Red poured again. Bryte said

"Easy Brett"

Brett asked Red instead of answering Bryte

"Where were you last night?"

"In my room, drank too much"

"Why were you drinking that much?"

"I was bored and had nothing to do. We have not invaded any valley in so many days"

"Why didn't you tell me that Elf could fight?"

Red took a sip and spoke

"She lived her life in Blue forest, she knows how to fight"

Brett yelled

"Get me some food"

Servants started serving food. They stayed quiet for a bit. Red asked

"Something happened?"

Brett said

"Renald is dead"

"Dead?"

"Yes, neck was slashed"

"How?"

"We do not know, Elf was in chains and chains were in bed"

"May be Renald took them off to enjoy the night with freedom"

Bryte laughed a little and Brett gave him a cold look. Bryte stopped.

"Renald's cloths were still on"

"May be Elf honey trapped him and made him believe that she is not going to do anything stupid"

Brett nodded

"I knew Renald since child hood, he was one of my best friends. I knew that he could not handle the Elf but still I gave her to him"

Red took a sip and said

"Well revenge is in your hands, cut her head off"

"She ran away in the night"

Red's hand stopped.

"Out of the castle, through the guards?"

"Yes, we went looking for her and swiped all the area but no luck"

"You know she is the key to contact the Balance, if she gets away then they will get help from the elves."

Brett was eating and said nothing. Red kept on drinking. Brett spoke again

"Adlard does not know anything, we will keep him in dark"

Red kept on sipping. Brett looked at him and said

"Keep the wine at bay, you are riding today"

"Me?"

"yes"

"Why?"

"You have to go after her, you have seen where she lives. She must not contact the Balance"

"There are only thirty elves in the forest, what are you afraid of?"

"Atlan confirmed that more passed through and more can come, u know that one elf just killed Renald while in chains and escaped our castle with guards on duty, we do not know if they know spells too or any special abilities, they are mythical creatures after all"

Red gave a sarcastic look and said

"First of all"

He threw up again. Servant quickly started cleaning up. Smell got bad again in the room.

Servant gave a wet cloth to Red and he wiped his mouth, he tried to pour more but Brett reached for the wine to take it away, Red gave him a cold look and he took back his hand, Red poured again. Brett said

"Bring him some water"

"What was I saying?"

"You said first of all and then you converted your words into vomit, I can't speak vomit"

"First of all, You saw the elf so now she is not mythical anymore, Elves are real and secondly they are not magical, they cannot do any spells"

"Well you are going, and that is done"

"Well if you insist, She will be in the forest before me"

"She have to go around Henry's valley cause Adlard's army is camping there, You can go through so time difference is even now"

Red drank a glass of water and stood up. Then he sat down again. Brett asked

"How much wine you had?"

"A lot, like a lot"

After an hour, Red was riding on his horse. He had his red armor on so he did not need to worry about Adlard's forces.

At Lord Clive's castle, They received the news that Elf escaped and Renald has been killed. Scouts were sent out to look for her. If more elves passed through the passage then they could help to win this war. Lord Nigel suggested that someone would go in the Blue Forest to contact the Balance. Jonald agreed to go with Ludik. Right now Ludik and Jonald were in the army camps and were looking at soldiers practicing. Jonald said

"First time in my life, I will go in the Blue forest"

"You scared?"

"Kind of, from child hood we were told to be afraid of the mountains and the forest. You chain an elephant to a post when it is a baby, it will try hardest to break free but post will be big enough to stop him. When the same elephant becomes adult, post is same but he does not even try because from childhood elephant's brain accept that post cannot be broken. If the elephant try even a little bit, it can break the post but it does not"

"That is why soldiers were scared to up to the mountains?"

"Yes, our brains have accepted that if we go there we die"

Soldiers made wooden big rhinos and were practicing to take them down with torches and long spears. They took one down and everybody chanted.

"So what we will do?"

"We have to go, and let's hope that elves are greater in numbers by now"

"How we will find them?"

"I have no idea, we need someone who can read trails and signs"

A soldier came running, He said to Jonald

"General, enemy platoon is seen west of here, They may be testers but you are ordered to take them down"

Jonald quickly stood up and asked Ludik

"Want to give them a test?"

Ludik smiled and sat on his horse. Jonald sat on his horse too and rode off. They were accompanied by Lord Nigel and General Riendo. Enemy were said to be in hundred. Testers were the first platoons sent to test the enemy. They were not to fight direct. Their first duty was recon. If nothing happens then set up a camp and if fight comes, they were to run back as quickly as they can. They took two hundred riders with them and at noon, they reached the enemy. Lord Nigel went towards the back with hundred riders so no one could escape. Jonald and Riendo went head on.

Enemy had started to make a camp. Their soldiers were busy in working and were not in any formation. Jonald and his rider ran them down from left side. Riendo and his riders ran them down from right side and Lord Nigel came from the back. It was a slaughter. They killed all the soldiers and only four ogres remained. Now was the test of their combat training. Riendo ordered soldiers to use new techniques which they were practicing. Horses started running. Ogres were growling and waving their cleavers. Riders started running at them. Their task was to hit them on vital organs or block their vision from the rider behind. If first rider was to block an attack or divert their attention.

Then second rider was to jump from his horse and go straight for the neck or heart. At first, ogres cut down some riders. Their cleavers were razor sharp. two riders got cut in two pieces. Then first ogre fell down with a rider on his chest. He pushed his sword straight into his heart. Then slowly, all ogres were killed. Jonald ordered to cut their heads off and take them back to show rest of the army. They all started riding back.

On the other side, Brett sent this platoon to only divert the attention. He and King Adlard invaded a neighboring valley. After reaching the valley, they found out that valley was evacuated including castle. There was no one in the valley but army set up so many booby traps that many men lost their lives trying to clear them up. Brett and King Adlard came back and ordered their army to clear the valley and castle.

It was a clear night, moon was full but blue forest was not letting any moon light through. Red rode fast and ran through the Blue Forest. He saw corpses of Ogres, trolls and big beasts lying in the forest here and there. He lost his horse to a beast attack. He climbed up a tree or he would have gotten killed too. Right now, he was sitting at the stream, hidden in the bushes. Stream water was flowing peacefully. Stream had no trees above it so water was looking like it is milk. Forest animals voices could be heard time to time. Red saw two elves drinking water from the stream before.

That is why Red was not crossing the stream. Both elves were male and once again they passed walking. Red figured that they were the guards. He spent the night in the bushes. At sunrise, Red saw many elves going in the opposite direction. Red had to find out if she was with them. Red quickly crossed the stream. He took the risk of being seen but no one did. He then took trees as cover and started moving behind them. They came a little far from Elf's tree house. Elves were walking in a single file formation so Red could not see all of them.

He followed them a little more but then he realized that it was pointless. If he tried to move forward then their rear guards would see him. He could not go around because it would take time to go without being seen. He did not know how long was their line. He could not climb a tree because their rear guards were turning around after every few steps. He decided to follow them until they make camp.

They will gather together and if Red could pass the guards then he could see if she was with them. After some more following he fell behind some steps because of the rear guards. They were walking real carefully now. Red had to take cover for more times. One time, he sneak a peek and saw that elves were gone. He could follow them but now he did not know when if guards were looking in his direction when he get them in his sight. He decided to walk back and wait for them back at the house. In case they come back but he had no choice. He started walking back. He heard a voice behind him

"There you are "

He turned around and saw Theia walking towards him. He quickly looked behind her but she was alone. Red ran his eyes on the surroundings but saw no one. Theia came close and smiled at him. Red just nodded and Theia started walking towards her tree. Red turned around and lifted his hand to punch. He decided to knock her out. Suddenly she turned around again and Red saw a letter in her hand. He started stretching his punching hand like he was tired. She turned around and gave the letter to him

"This is for you"

Red saw that it was sealed. Elf started walking again. Red opened the letter and saw the writing

"Consider this my last favor, Brother"

Red took a deep breath and tore the letter. He started walking behind the Elf and started dropping letter pieces one by one. They walked silently until they reached her tree. Red had the last piece in his hand. He stood there and looked at the last piece. Then he dropped it. His hand went to his dagger handle.

"What happened?" asked Theia. She came close to him again and her big blue eyes gazed him in his eyes. Red's hand came off the handle.

"Isn't this your place?"

"Not anymore, I changed it"

"Where?"

"A little more deep. close to where I sent you off to deep forest"

Red started walking. Elf was walking beside him. They came to stream and turned their way to the deep forest. Soft sunshine was lighting up the stream. Water was flowing with a soft sound. Red was walking silent. He was looking at his feet along side Theia's feet. His hand went to his dagger couple of times but came down again. Theia noticed it and asked

"Why are you reaching for your dagger? habit?"

"No, Other elves are in this area and they can attack me"

Theia laughed. It was first time Red heard her laugh. Red looked at her laughing face and a smile came on his face.

"I am with you, they will not attack you"

Her sentence 'I am with you', hammered Red's mind over and over again. Forest sounds faded away and only thing Red could hear was this sentence. He kept on walking without noticing anything. His hands started to sweat.

"We have to turn this way"

Forest sounds came back to Red. Theia was showing him the way. He followed her. They turned with the stream. After more walking, they came to Theia's new tree. Same old picture but this time it was hidden in tree branches. They climbed up the tree and Red saw all her old stuff. A sparrow nest was new. Sparrow saw Red and flew away. Theia said

"You scared it. birds are not afraid of elves. They sit on my hand all the time"

Red smiled. This was new to him. His smiles were very rare.

"You are magical after all"

"No, I would not say magical but birds like me"

Red sat on the edge of her platform. She sat beside him. They said nothing. Wind howled and Theia's hair whipped Red on his face. Theia grabbed her hair and said

"Sorry"

They went silent again. Then Theia said

"Thanks for saving me"

"hmmmmm"

Wind howled again. Theia grabbed her hair. Red stared at her face. She knew that he was staring. Her cheeks started to blush. Red knew she was stopping a smile. He just wanted her to smile like she did in the forest earlier. Her face was looking golden by sunlight. Her blue eyes were sparkling and it was clear that she was happy. She looked at him from the corner of her eye and quickly went back to looking straight. Red asked

"What is your name?"

"Theia"

"Beautiful name"

"Thank you, yours?"

"Red"

"I meant Real name"

Red went silent. He forgot his name. He was Red shadow for so much time that he forgot his own name.

"no worries if you do not want to tell"

"I forgot my name"

Theia laughed and then looked at Red, He was serious.

"How is this possible?"

"When you do not get called by your name for twenty years, it can happen"

"I lived alone my whole life but I did not forgot mine"

"You lived in one place, you had memories but I had nothing. Just hide and seek with law"

"I will call you Red then"

Red nodded. He kept on looking straight. Theia asked

"Where is your family?"

"They are dead, when I was a child"

"Mine too"

"You got more elves, you can go back with them"

"I cannot, my father told me that there is nothing where we came from. Just darkness. There is no light, no living. it is like a long sleep. When first battle was fought. After the battle my father liked this life and chose to stay here. He liked a woman elf during war and they both lived here."

"But first war happened centuries ago"

"Yes, my parents were pure Elves, They did not age like humans do. My father told me that my one year was equal to twenty years of humans. My father and mother slept for many years that sometimes landscape changed when they woke up. It was because their bodies were used to sleep forever.

Then I was born. I aged according to elf years and when I was eight years old. My mother died. I do not remember the reason. When I was ten years old. My father died too because of sickness. Our bodies were adapting human place. My father tried to teach me everything he knew. I learned fighting from him. Making stuff, morals and language of humans. After my father died. I started to age like humans"

Red was listening to this fairy tale. He had nothing to say. She asked

"Why do you kill innocents?"

"No one is innocent Theia, Everybody do bad things. Some in darkness of night and some behind closed doors"

"But they do not hurt anyone"

"I was hurt, my family was hurt. Every person I kill gives me happiness and some revenge"

Theia stared at him. He had pain on his face. He turned his face towards her. She had questions in her eyes. Red sighed and said

"My father was a soldier in Henry's army. Henry is the lord I killed in this forest and it was the start where I got involved in this matter. Henry and Artis fought. My father died protecting

Henry from some enemies. Henry escaped death and later hr defeated Artis. My mother had nothing. Only me and my younger brother. My mother went to the castle many times to ask for help but no one allowed her in. She started to work in houses as a servant.

I was six years old and my brother was four years old. One day my mother came crying to home. Her clothes were ripped. A man in whose home my mother worked, raped her. My mother tried take help from law but that man was powerful. He told everybody that my mother tried to seduce him to get money and when he refused, she accused him. Nobody did anything. After that, my mother used her savings to raise us but she did not had much.

She taught us to read and write. Nobody gave her job because ladies of the houses gossiped and no woman wanted a seducer in her house and near her man. After our savings ran out, my mother sat alone one night. She did not talk to us. Next morning, I saw a man come to our home and he spent some time behind closed door with my mother. After he left, mother gave me money to get food supplies. Then this became a routine. When me and my brother went out. People would say that we are the brothel kids. Then I knew that my mother became a prostitute. She was selling her body to raise us. I tried to work. Nobody wanted to give a job to a seven year old boy who was son of a prostitute.

One day, a mob of men came to our house. They were yelling and demanding that my mother leave the valley. My mother did not have enough money to move. They took our house and pushed us to a house which was on the edge of the houses. My mother would send us out to play when any man came. I knew what was happening and I think my brother too. But we were kids and we were happy because we use to run in the open plains and play all day.

We both use to play with only each other because other kid's parents would not allow them to play with us. We were sons of a fighter, we would play sword fighting all day. At night, when we returned, my mother would tell us stories to put us to sleep because clients had to come at night too. Sometimes, when any man would leave, I woke up and see their faces. I saw the same faces which were in the mob which took our house and pushed us at the edge. These were those respectable men who could not bear a prostitute in their respectable town."

Red stopped. Theia was listening. She felt sorry for Red. She asked

"Is your mother alive?"

"No, when I was eleven years old. my mother got sick. We tried take care of her. But her health went down too quick. At the point where she could not even stand. She laid in bed all day. My brother use to cry with her. I use to cook and keep her clean. She always said 'You are the sons of a honorable man, let nobody disrespect you'. Her mental health went low too.

She was becoming a living skeleton. She could not eat and only could drink liquids. I could not see her in this condition. Her words changed near her death. She would say to us "You are sons of a honorable man but Your mother is a prostitute, earn back your respect". She did not like how she wasted her life. Then she died"

A tear was making its way down Red's cheek. Theia said "I am sad for you Red"

Red wiped the tear off. Theia waited some time and then said "Your brother?"

"After my mother, we did not know what to do. We had little money but how long could we survive? We both traveled to other valley. It was near Crystal sea. Nobody knew us there. We spent four years there. Sometimes doing small jobs and sometimes begging. One time, we got caught stealing and fled the valley to save our heads. We came back to Henry's valley. Everybody had forgotten us. They did not see our faces for ten years.

Six years at the edge of the valley and four years without our mother. We changed a lot. We used different names and told made up stories to justify from where we came. We did not tell anyone that we were brothers. One day in the market, Henry came. When he was getting off the horse. His crown fell off. I quickly grabbed it and ran. I came to the tavern where my brother lived and told him everything. I stayed hidden while my brother went out to see the situation.

He came back and told me that Henry is offering a big reward to anyone who could get back the crown. I did not want to give back because I hated Henry and this was his family signature. But my brother said that we cannot sell it anywhere and we needed proper money to set a life. He returned the crown and made a fake story. We divided the money. My brother bought a house but we both did not know any kind of work but only fighting.

Our whole lives, we ran, fought and stole. I used money to buy weapons. We both became hired killers. After that, my life changed, I did not saw anything in the contracts. Poor, rich, innocent or not innocent. I killed everyone. I once killed ten men in one night. That's why my name got famous and I hid in the shadows forever. They now say that if sun is red in the morning, it means that I killed someone"

Red laughed. Theia smiled too. She felt a little relieved that Red was laughing. She asked

"Who was your first kill?"

"My mother"

"What?" Theia asked in shock.

"On her last night, my mother was in so much pain that she could not speak. She had this pain for many days but that night it crossed her limits. She was trying to say something but her voice could not reach me. I moved near her and placed my ear on her mouth. She said "Kill me, free me". I looked at her with tears. She was crying too. I placed my hands on her neck and started to press. I was crying but my mother smiled at me in her final breath. Then her soul left her body"

Theia did not know what to say. They both were listening to forest sounds. After a while, Red stood up, he said

"I will be going now Theia"

"Where you going?"

"Back to Brett's castle, I never found you. You reached elves before I could"

Theia had a confused look on her face. She could not understand what Red was saying.

"But you sent that man to get me out of that castle "

"I did not, He was my brother. He knows me. He was at the castle last night "

"Then why are you here? He said that you will come to meet me"

"I was sent to catch you again before you can contact the elves. He killed one of Brett's best and oldest friends"

One more time Red let her down. She was happy that Red cared about her which gave her some clues about her own feelings too.

"You broke my trust again Red"

"I did not, I never asked anyone to save you. He was at the castle last night and I returned to my room very drunk. I must have said something while drunk"

Wind howled. Red was standing and Theia was sitting.

"What did you say?"

"I was drunk, I cannot remember"

"What was in the letter?"

"He figured out something which I could not. That is why he saved you"

"What did he figured out?"

"Me"

Then Red turned around and started walking towards the tree. He reached the trunk but Theia's hand held his arm. She was standing behind him.

"You said you were here to capture me"

"Yes"

"You didn't"

"I couldn't"

She came in front of him. It was first time that she was so close to him.

"You are going back to fight a war Red, They are killing innocent people"

"I am one of them, I killed innocent people my whole life"

"You were hurt Red, These people are not. They just want new lands and wealth"

"Contact the elves Theia, They moved to the direction from where I was coming from today. Do what you feel right and I will do what feels right to me"

Theia left his arm and he climbed down. He started walking fast as he needed to cover a lot of distance.

20

CHAPTER 20

Brett, King Adlard and Atlan were sitting with Red. Red was telling them "She got to elves before I reached her. I saw her moving with them."

Brett: How many elves?

Red: I do not know, They were moving in a line and Forest is too dense to tell. Their rear guards were looking back every few steps.

Atlan: King asks any direction?

Red: They were moving more deep but now Theia is with them so they will be moving to enemies aid.

Brett: Well now we have to prepare.

Red: I lost my spy.

Brett: Caught?

Red: No, he was at this castle before I went after the elf. He left me a letter saying this is his last favor.

Brett: pity, he gave us useful information. Renald only gave us three pieces of information. Your guy gave us everything we know about their army. Why the sudden change?

Red: Cannot say anything. I saw no changes in behavior.

Brett stood up.

"let us go to troops, we need to go forward"

They all stood up.

At Lord Clive's castle, Elves came. Theia brought them with her. Males and female elves were all fighters. They were around five hundred. Theia was standing with Lords. They were watching soldiers doing combat practice. Elves were more faster than human soldiers. It took twenty soldiers to bring down a wooden rhino but it only took eight elves to bring down the rhino. Lords were very grateful to Theia for doing this. Their commander name Kerk and the old elf who was translating named Poif.

Clive: What do you guys do in the other world?

Poif translated and Kerk replied. Poif translated to Lord Clive

Kerk: It is a sleep, other world is just a spell. We are created by magic. Many of us were in the first battle.

Artis: So how do you know all of this?

Kerk laughed.

"We just do, I cannot explain it but we know."

Nigel: Well it is a great help, you are stronger than us humans.

Kerk: It is our only purpose. We came out the passage. I was the first one so they made me their commander. I fought with Draound in the battle. He was a great man.

Artis: Scouts report that Henry's valley is getting evacuated. We do not know where they are moving. But they are getting ready to attack.

Philip: They still have more men then us.

Artis: What Generals told us, it indicates that they have no sense of fighting the formations. We can take them.

Kerk: It will be a battle with great blood shed but we have to fight.

Clive: We have to set formations, and try to spread the army so their fireballs can not do much damage.

Philip: General who saw them is trying to recreate them in the armory.

Artis: Any luck?

Philip: meh.

Nigel: They do not have horses. Our mounted squads can do some serious damage.

Artis: yes, Jonald and you were able to slaughter their testers with ease.

Kerk: You should make some squads to just run through them. They do not stop for anything. no formations. just running and killing.

Clive: That is a good idea.

Jonald and Ludik joined them.

Clive: How are soldiers looking General?

Jonald: They are ready for battle My lord, confidence is up and after seeing the elves joining our side, their courage is more strong.

Nigel: Also after you brought back the heads of the ogres.

Artis: That was good decision General.

Jonald: We had to show soldiers that they are not as strong as we thought.

Clive: You are quite popular in the soldiers.

Jonald: I am just doing my Job My lord.

Exercises were complete and soldiers were leaving the training grounds and sun was going down. Jonald and Ludik left with the soldiers. Kerk ,Poif and Theia left with the elves. Lords came back to the castle. Night was upon them.

Lord Clive and Lord Artis sat in the study room so they can receive more scout reports. Tensions were high as enemy was moving out of Henry's valley.

Ludik and Jonald came to a group of soldiers who were sitting around a fire and playing music. Soldiers saw Jonald and welcomed him with loud chants and happy faces. They offered them wine which was accepted. Soldiers skinned the skulls of the ogres and placed them on poles to set around army camps. One was standing here too. Soldiers requested Jonald to tell them the story of how they slaughter the testers. This happened almost every night, Jonald went around the camp and every time soldiers would ask him. Jonald was indeed popular among the soldiers.

When Theia reached Elvish camp, all were asleep. Poif told Theia that ELves had no concept of entertainment. Guards will wake them up in the morning or they will sleep for years. Kerk offered her a tent but Theia did not want to sleep. She apologized and came back to her room.

At the same time, on the edge of the army camps, Rio entered his tent. He saw Red sitting in his tent. Red was wearing Rio's armor which was all muddy. Rio closed the tent's gate flaps and asked

"What are you doing here?"

"No brother, what are you doing here?"

Rio sighed and sat on his bed.

"I am in service of Lord Philip now"

"Why?"

"He offered me a job on a high post and I took it"

"Why?"

"He have a lot of warriors in his service, he heard about me killing an ogre. First record kill so he offered me to join him"

"That's it? he offered you a job and you took it? threw all the wealth and lands which Brett promised?"

"Yes"

"Why?"

"to earn my respect"

Red understood.

"We will get respect on the winning side too"

"That is not respect, they are invading"

"Invasions happen"

"Have you ever had the taste of true respect? when I walk in the camp now, Soldiers offer me drinks and call my name with their pure hearts because I am helping to save their lands and lives, on your side they will give me respect too but I am helping them to get wealth. economical benefit"

Rio was smiling, Red said

"They will lose, Brett has a larger army"

"Mother said, earn your respect. We are not children of killers. Our father was soldier and a good man"

"Father died proving that and mother is also not around anymore"

Rio just lifted his shoulders. Red asked

"What changed you all of a sudden?"

"Join me and see for yourself, all of our lives we were nothing. People would hate us or fear us. Now, people praise me. They give me importance"

"You got your gang with you?"

"Na, half of them were killed by your forces and only two survived. I found them here."

"hmmm"

Rio asked

"You came here to ask me this?"

"Yes, when the battle comes, stay away from me. I do not want to kill one more of my family members"

Rio started laughing.

"I am a better fighter then you"

"So that is why people fear me more then you, oh wait, now They 'RESPECT' you "

They both laughed. Rio said

"Second level and third door to the right. Shifts will change soon and you got some time to enter, I don't think getting out will be a problem"

"I came for something else"

"Well you are here, plus you are dying in the battle anyways because I will be looking for you"

Red stood up smiling, he reached for the flaps but before going out. He asked

"What is my name?"

Rio had a confused look, they heard Rio's gang members coming. Red got out. He walked around the camps which took him a lot of time. He had to sneak past the guards. He reached for the castle's backdoor. No one was there. He picked up the wine barrel of the guards and placed it on his shoulder. He was wearing Rio's armor so there was no problem. He walked through the halls and went up the stairs. Shifts were changing so no guards were present. He got on the second floor and on the third door, he knocked. After some time, door opened a little and Theia was peeking. She saw Red and opened the door fully. She was wearing a blue gown. Her hair were untied. She whispered worriedly

"What are you doing here Red?"

"Came to deliver this wine"

"What are you talking about?"

They heard armor clanking. She quickly grabbed Red's arm and pulled him inside. Theia closed the door. Red placed the barrel on the floor in a corner. Theia placed her ear on the door. Red turned around and stood silent. A window was open and moon light was coming in the room. After the voices faded. Theia turned around, anger and worry could be seen in her eyes.

"What are you doing in the castle?"

"Told you, came to deliver the wine"

"I do not drink wine"

"uh oh, I brought the wrong order"

Red looked at the wine jug on her table which was full. He poured some and drank it. Theia just looked at him. He poured again and drank it with one gulp. He looked at Theia and she raised her arms in a question gesture. He poured again and lifted the glass. Theia came forward and snatched the glass away. She placed it on the table. Red tried to reach for it but she took the glasses and jug to her side table. She placed them there and turned around. Red was smiling. Theia felt her anger going away. She asked

"I am going to ask you one more time, what are you doing here?"

"Night reminds me of your hair, came to see them"

Theia sighed. He was not in the mood to answer questions. She sat on the bed.

"You are not happy to see me?"

She placed her hands on her forehead and started rubbing.

"I am but in the castle? you can get caught and they will kill you"

"worth it"

She lifted her head up and saw that Red was wearing their colors. A hope came to her.

"You joined us?"

His head moved from left to right. Hope died.

"Then why are you wearing our colors? and why are you in bad condition?"

"Had to sneak in"

"Why is your armor all muddy and yourself, Your face is dirt and hairs are all over your face"

"I rode all day to get here, my face is dusty and it is called a beard. I could not shave for sometime"

Red's beard grew. He did not shave for a month. Theia stood up and went out. Red sat there quietly. He was feeling a little happy that she was worried. This was new to him. After some time, he stood up and went to pour wine. Door opened and Theia came in.

"No wine Red"

"My mouth is dry"

"There is water here"

Red turned around and saw Theia with shave foam in a bowl and a beard knife. He asked

"What is that for?"

"Cut your hair, you do not look good with bard"

"Beard"

"Whatever"

Red came to his chair again. Theia placed the bowl and knife on the table. Red poured some water and drank it. Theia asked

"Did you eat? anything?"

"I did, do not worry"

Theia sat on the bed again.

"I was going to sleep just right now but I did not feel sleepy"

"I disturbed you?"

"No, no"

Red smiled and Theia looked down smiling. She said

"I will be very sad if they kill you"

"They will not catch me Theia"

"What if they do?"

"I will take many with me to hell"

"Hell?"

"Bad people go to hell after dying, good people go to heaven. Hell is filled with fire and punishment forever."

"Then do good stuff, go to heaven. What is in heaven?"

Red smiled.

"Heaven is filled with wine and beautiful lands. never end-ing"

"How is this possible?"

"Long story"

Theia saw that Red is staring at her. She blushed. She said

"How will you go back?"

"Let me worry about it"

"I am worried for you"

Red stood up and came to the window. He looked out and then said

"You know why I have feelings for you?"

Theia felt very happy, Red just told her that he have feelings for her. She asked

"Why?"

"Because you give me the feelings which I did not even know that I needed"

"But you captured me, punched me and not once. couple of times"

Red laughed. Theia smiled embarrassingly. Red turned around and looked at her. She said

"I never met any man, my father was the last person. After all this matter started, I saw many men but what I feel about you is I cannot explain. All the people around me but I only think about you in a special way. I worry about you. When someone talks about you bad, I feel bad. My breath go heavy when they talk about killing you. You are in front of me right now and I am sweating"

Red smiled.

"This is called love Theia"

"How do you know that you love me?"

"Because you are the only person who snatched away that wine glass from my hand and I did not feel angry about it. No one is allowed to do that"

Theia's heart was jumping in her chest. She felt her feet and hands getting cold.

"My hands are cold"

Red came forward and placed his hand on her forehead. Theia felt a chill in her body.

"You are just overwhelmed. Too many feelings. Breath"

Red sat on his chair again. Theia did not know what to do now. She said

"You have to cut your beard"

"I am fine, I do not want to right now"

"Do it" "I will when I go back"

"Like you are doing it for past days"

Theia stood up and took the bowl. She took some foam and started brushing Red's face. Red resisted but she did it anyway. Then she took the knife.

"I can do it on my own"

"Let me"

"You will cut me"

"I will not let that happen"

Theia smiled at Red. Pure love and happiness could be seen on her face. Red sat quietly. She started shaving Red's face very carefully. Her blue eyes were focused and her breath was hitting Red's face. Red felt her fingers on his face when she held his face. She was moving the beard knife very slowly and very carefully. She said with a smile.

"Red"

"Hmm?"

"Is there any other time you did something bad to me? like you captured me and punched me"

"Well, I helped someone to capture you"

"Who?"

"Lord Philip's soldiers, when they were sitting on your tree. Those idiots fell asleep. I was sitting on a tree top. First I had to place your canteen in the way to get them to you and then you tried to escape after waking up, I threw an apple on captain's face to wake him up. It was a long shot but luckily it hit him on his face and they were able to capture you"

Theia stopped her hand and looked at Red angrily. Red lifted his shoulders. She started the shave again.

"I should cut your neck Red. You are in my reach right now" She laughed.

Red smiled and said

"Then who will you love?"

Theia felt so happy. There is someone who care about her. She finished the shave. Red stood up and said

"It is time for me to go Theia"

"Will you come back?"

"cannot say"

"Just don't die Red"

"I won't but you don't come to any battle, go back to your tree. After all this, I will find you"

Red walked out. He saw Jonald and Ludik knocking on a door. Door opened and they went in. He knocked on Theia's door again. Theia opened a little. He asked

"I came to meet you, but will you be angry if I work too?"

"What do you mean?"

"I am in enemies' castle, I can do a lot of work here"

"No, Red no working tonight"

"Please?"

"I said no"

"Just a little"

"No killings, no work"

Then she said

"Wait"

She walked away and came back with a glass of wine.

"If you do not kill anyone, you can have one glass of wine"

Red took the glass with a smile, Theia closed the door and Red started walking towards the room where Jonald and Ludik went. He drank the wine and placed the glass on the door. He placed his ear on the glass and started hearing faded voices.

Jonald: We are through the battle plan. Now you will be in court.

Artis: Past is past Jonald, I am helping now.

Jonald: What you did is not forgivable.

Artis: You need me, nobody will punish me.

Jonald: Let us see. we will move day after tomorrow. Same time, tomorrow night. I will get you to Lords and tell them everything.

Red walked back and started humming the tune he always hums. He walked down the stairs when Jonald and Ludik passed him. Jonald said

"Do not make sound soldier, everyone is asleep"

Red nodded and stopped the humming. He came out of the castle and walked straight into army camp. If Jonald did not notice anything then no one would.

21

CHAPTER 21

Brett and Adlard were riding on horses. Adlard did not know how to ride and nor did Atlan. They were riding slow. Their army was making its way to Lord Clive's valley. This was the final battle. After that, it would not be hard to take the whole land. It was taking times because of Adlard's army was on foot and their fireball structures were slow to move. Brett's army had done all they could to teach Adlard's army to fight formations effectively. Brett's testers made camps at three locations. They were moving to one of those camps. Brett was telling Adlard about his father.

Brett: One time, a king came from outside, He had an army and thought that he could take Land of Draound. All lords got together and my father had the command of the army. He defeated that King. My father is a hot headed man. He fought other lords too. He has the most experience. At the battle field, try to kill my father first. He can do some serious damage to us.

Adlard: I will order my soldiers.

Brett: Other one is Philip. He fought with my father too. He has all the great fighters in his command. His men can kill many of us.

Adlard: We have many to spare.

Brett: Lord Clive, he is a mind master. He will be playing all the tricks in this battle. We do not have any danger from him physically.

Adlard: Half the battle is won through mind Brett. Do not underestimate him.

At Lord Clive's, army was moving out. Orders were getting yelled. Soldiers were walking and packing tents. Whole village of tents in front Lord Clive's castle was getting packed. Horses were running here and there. Generals were instructing their men to hurry up. Enemy was at move. Elves were marching too and Kerk was in charge of them. Lords were figuring out last details of the battle plan. Till noon, they was only a small part of army left, Lords were to go tomorrow. Generals went with the soldiers but Jonald stayed.

Ludik knew what he wanted to do so he stayed too. Lord Artis knew why he stayed but he was confident that nothing will happen to him. He was a experienced lord and Clive was his friend. At this valley, Lord Clive's orders were to be carried out. Philip can make a problem but Nigel was his friend too. Votes were equal but situation was in his favor. No one can make rash decisions in the time.

Theia went with the elves. She wanted to do her part in the battle. Every pair of hands were needed which can fight. Rio and his two friends went with Lord Philip's soldiers. Rio was happy with his new life. At night, Lord Clive received the reports that enemy was moving in his direction. He sent this news to army. All lords sat together for final time and discussed the situation. After that, they all went to rooms. They were to move early in the morning. Lord Artis came to his room. He drank a glass of wine and there was a knock on the door. He knew Jonald was here. He opened and saw Jonald standing.

Jonald: Let's go.

Artis: I am still a Lord, say my lord.

Jonald: You are not a lord, you lost your valley, your son and you are a murderer.

Artis: Nothing will happen Jonald, why go through this?

Jonald: We will see.

Artis: Where are the other Lords?

Jonald: Ludik is calling them to study room.

Artis sighed. He walked out and Jonald gave him the way. As soon as he came out, a powerful punch knocked him out. He saw nothing and went blank. His eyes opened a little after sometime. He saw Ludik in front of him. He was lying in the hall way. He saw Lord Clive, Lord Philip and Ludik. He stood up with support of the wall. His head was spinning. Ludik saw him and quickly grabbed his arm to support him. Lord Artis walked to Lord Clive and behind him he saw his room's door open. Jonald was laying down and a knife was in his heart. Blood was still coming out of his chest. On the wall, it was written

"This one is on the house Lord Artis"

This was the work of Red, he remembered the night when he asked Red to kill Jonald. Lord Clive asked

"What happened Artis?"

"I do not know, Jonald gave me the way to come to you but someone knocked me out"

"Ludik called us, he found Lord Nigel dead in his room. His wine was poisoned"

Ludik said

"My lords, I saw a man when I came here. He was trying to wake up Lord Artis. He saw me and ran when I yelled for the guards"

They all came to throne room. Lord Artis was given water. He told them everything. from start to the end. His mind was not working properly but he managed to complete his story. Lord Philip said

"This is bad Artis, you did worse thing possible"

"I know, I was ready to face the trial"

"There will be no trial"

Lord Artis looked at Philip with surprise. Lord Clive and Ludik did the same thing. Philip was the one who hated Artis most. Lord Clive said

"Why Philip?"

"Because soldiers loved Jonald, now he is dead and if we punish Artis then it would send the wrong message that we are fighting among ourselves. Soldiers need courage and what good is a dead General and a punished Lord? Artis experience can save all of our lives and families. One murder can be forgiven for saving thousand lives"

Lord Artis tears gather up in his eyes. He felt very ashamed for what he did to Henry. He started crying. He said

"I am sorry for what I did, I did wrong"

Ludik quickly grabbed water and gave it to Lord Artis. Lord Artis started drinking. Lord Clive said

"We need each other right now, we need to be unite and ready"

In the morning, they started their ride. Lord Philip instructed Ludik to tell the officers to tell soldiers that Red assassinated Jonald and now they have to avenge Jonald's death.

Brett and Adlard were sitting in a tent along with Atlan and Bryte. Red walked in. He was shaved and wearing his red armor. Brett said

"Where were you Red?"

"Easing up your problems"

"What do you mean?"

Red sat down and reached for the wine but then he stopped for a second and reached for the water.

"You know Jonald?"

"No"

He poured some water and drank it.

"New General, Henry's army"

"Oh yeah, he rode down our testers and is popular among their soldiers, I was telling Adlard to watch out for that man"

"He is no more a man, he is a soul now"

"You killed him?"

"Bye bye General, welcome to heaven"

Brett started laughing. He poured glasses of wine for everyone and everyone lifted except Red. Brett asked

"You will not cheer?"

"I gave up wine"

"Why?"

Red lifted his shoulders but then he lifted his water glass. They all cheered and drank.

"You know Lord Nigel?"

"Dead?"

"Bye Bye Lord, time to meet your daughter and sons"

Brett poured again. They all cheered again. Brett and Adlard were very happy. Adlard said something and Atlan translated.

"Red can have a boggart and any woman he choose from my army"

"Boggart?" Red asked.

"Big rhino things" Brett replied.

Red nodded. Then Brett told Bryte to tell this news to the army. Adlard asked Red to tell the story and Red told them.

Brett: You could have done my father too.

Red: A soldiers saw me, I was waking him up to see Jonald. After all, it was his assignment.

They all laughed. It was a good news and it could weaken their army a little. They were just a day march away from battle. After some time, Red walked out with Atlan towards Adlard's army. He had women in his army too. Many were just medics but some were warriors too. He saw Bryte and asked him to join him. Bryte was a little surprised. They all walked through Adlard's army. Red asked Bryte

"If you were me, what kind of woman would you choose?"

"well, I have been with medics before but fighter woman are new thing to me. I would definitely try one of them"

Atlan ordered all woman fighters to gather around. They were many. Red asked Bryte

"I am having a hard time choosing Bryte, Help a brother out"

Bryte was confused by Red's behavior but he looked at all the girls. He found one who was very beautiful. She was wielding a sword and had plump lips. Her hair were brown and eyes were black. He pointed at her. Atlan said something in his language. Girl came forward. Red said

"You have quite an eye Bryte"

Bryte laughed. A man came forward too. Atlan said

"He is her brother, he demands to know who is taking her"

Red pushed Bryte forward.

"He is taking her on your King's command"

Bryte was surprised. He was feeling a little envy for Red for getting such a girl. Girl came forward and said something. Atlan translated

"She said that she will be good to you and protect you from all harm"

Red laughed and turned around. Atlan joined him while Bryte was getting congratulated by Adlard's army in their own language.

At noon, Lords reached their army. Messengers were sent before they arrived to Brett to meet for negotiations. He accepted and Lords rode forward without any guards. Theia, Poif and Kerk joined them. They reached the tent in the afternoon. They entered and saw Brett, Adlard, Bryte, Atlan and Red sitting. Chairs were empty on the opposite side. They all sat. Artis was looking angrily at Brett.

Atlan: What are your propositions?

Philip: Leave the land and go back.

Atlan: That is not a way.

Clive: Then let us show you your way back.

Brett: Uncle, we have the numbers and strength. You can not win.

Clive: Do not call me uncle, you are a disgrace.

Brett: This disgrace got you on your knees uncle.

Artis: We are not on our knees boy, we can end this war with no blood spilled.

Adlard: My people are ready to bleed.

Artis: You can go back, or go beyond the Miller's pass. If you stay here then we have no choice but to send you all to hell.

Adlard laughed.

Artis: Do you have propositions?

Adlard: Give us the land, We will let your people live here under my rule. Your armies will be mine and we will go beyond to conquer more lands.

Philip: We are not slaves, we will fight till our last breath. We defeated you before when you ran back like rats and it took you long enough to come back.

Adlard: Times change, weapons change. What we did to your forces in the first valley, They looked like rats when running.

Artis: Times do change. Lets see if you will be running your mouth after the battle.

Adlard: There is another way.

Clive: What is it?

Adlard: Give me the this she elf and I will give you more days to live.

Red fist clenched. Theia noticed. They both were sitting opposite of each other on the corner chairs.

Clive: She is our companion. We do not trade companions as slaves.

Adlard: I will return her. She will not be able to walk though.

Artis: If you want no negotiations, we will be going. See you at war.

They all stood up. Artis stopped for a second and slapped Brett from across the table. Swords came out all of a sudden. Brett said

"Relax everybody, Relax. My father is angry and as a father he have right to slap me"

Artis: What about you Bryte? you did not stop him from this madness?

Bryte: I am just his bodyguard, I cannot say anything.

Artis: With that mentality, You will always be a guard.

Bryte said nothing. Swords went back. Red gave way in a manner that his back came in front of Theia. Theia was standing so nobody could see from behind. Adlard, Atlan, Bryte and Brett walked out. Red gave a paper to Theia and walked out. Nobody saw this. Then they all walked out and got on their horses. During the ride, Theia opened the letter.

"There is a pond to your camp right, between the trees. I heard that I can see two nights at a time"

Theia smiled. He was talking about her hair. They kept on riding.

At night, Theia took her horse and rode to the direction which Red told her in the letter. She kept on looking back in case she was getting followed. After riding for some time, She came upon a grove. She tied her horse to a tree and walked in. After coming in the middle, She saw a pond in between. Trees were not covering the pond so the moon light was making a circle around it. Theia stood still because she knew that Red was standing behind her.

"You do not have to sneak up on me Red"

"Habits"

Red came in front. His eyes and smile showed love. He took Theia's hand and walked up to the Pond. They sat with holding hands.

"I heard you killed a General in the castle"

"And a lord too"

"I told you not to kill"

"You told me not kill that night, I killed them when you left the castle"

"Red, this is bad na"

"There are two sides, bad and good. For you good are innocent people, for me good are people who pay me better than the other"

"We can pay you too"

"I have made a commitment my love"

"hush"

"What?"

"Why are you calling me my love?, someone will hear"

Red started laughing and Theia realized her mistake. There was no one here except them. Then Red said

"Why you came here? I told you to go far from the war"

"I wanted to do my part"

"You already did, you brought the elves"

"Every fighter is needed"

"Come on Theia, what if you get killed?"

"What if you get killed?"

"It is my job, I am in the army"

"Now it is my job too, I am in the army too"

"I should tie you here until the war is over"

Theia smiled and leaned a bit towards him. She opened her eyes a little more and looked him in the eyes.

"Ask yourself if you can do it"

Red just smiled. Theia said again

"May be I should do this to you"

"well, Ask yourself if you can do it"

"I can do anything to protect you from harm"

Red laughed.

"What?"

"Nothing"

"Red"

"I am just happy that I have a protector"

Theia laughed too. A leaf broke from a tree and flew. It came down on Red's head. Theia left his hand and brushed his hair to get the leaf out. She felt happy and good. She kept on brushing his hair with hand. Red put his chin on his knuckles.

"My brother is fighting from your side Theia"

Theia kept on brushing.

"Guards are too many, I can not sneak pass them. Can you give him my message? He is the only family I have left"

"Yes"

"Tell him, not to come to war. Tell him to take you to your tree. I will find you both"

"I am not going anywhere Red, And if he is your brother then he will not go too. I can tell that by looking at you. You are not willing to come with me"

"Your army will lose Theia, They will slaughter everyone"

"So be it"

Red said nothing. Theia kept on brushing. After some time, Red stood up.

"You should go Theia, if you return late then they will suspect that you are a spy"

Theia stood up. They came to her horse.

"Ask for Rio, he is in Philip's service. Do not tell anyone that he is my brother. It will create problems for him"

"Do not worry Red, I will not"

"I will wait for you here, same time"

"I will come, I promise"

Red kissed her hand. She got on her horse and said

"You know, I saw humans kissing lips too. I do not think you love me enough"

Red laughed and Theia smiled.

"Next time"

She nodded and turned her horse. Red saw her riding away. She came back to the camp and found Rio. She gave him the message. Then she went to her tent to sleep.

22

CHAPTER 22

Next morning, when the sun came up. Both armies started marching. Clanking of armors could be heard and marching footsteps were making the ground shiver. Drums were banging. Riders were riding their horses and scouts were looking out for ambush. Tensions were high. Lords were riding together and discussing the situation. Ludik was the in charge of the new horse squad. Philip's new bodyguard was Rio. He was riding silently with them.

Artis: We need to attack their officers. We have less numbers so better cut the heads of the army.

Clive: This will bring courage to our army.

Philip: Shadow death is not an officer but he is a sign of terror too. If we can kill him then we will gain benefit.

Artis: Now we have seen his face, we can target him too.

Clive: I have instructed long bows to aim for the fireballs throwers.

Kerk: My elves will be looking for ogres and boggarts. Horse squads can distract enemy.

Philip: Brett army should have prepared Adlard's people to fight the proper formations. It will be not as easy as last time.

Artis: All we can do is wait and fight. Lets see what happens.

A little late in the afternoon, they came to the fighting grounds. They could see the enemy camping far away. As soon as they reached, enemy started moving forward. Officers started yelling orders. Soldiers took formations. Lords separated to different locations in the army. Enemy halted at one chalk. Lord Clive ordered to bring forward the shields. Shielded soldiers came forwards and formed a line. Everyone went silent. Then they saw Brett coming forward and he took out his sword. Enemy soldiers started running towards them. Archers knocked their arrows.

When enemy came to half chalk. Archers released the arrows. Arrows came down like rain on enemy. Enemy started falling. But from behind them came Boggarts. Enemy soldiers were riding them. Boggarts could easily run through the shields. Boggarts were followed by more enemy soldiers. From right, came Ludik with his horse squads. Some horses were rode by elves. Ludik swarmed them and elves jumped on the Boggarts. Horse squads were coming in small groups. They rode down the following enemies and they started running back.

Elves quickly took down the Boggarts. And horsemen picked them while running. They did not stop. First wave was ineffective. Soldiers started yelling in happiness. After some time and regrouping, second wave of the enemy made their way to them. This time, it had ogres and humans. Archers did the same thing but this time specific archers had steel headed arrows and they were aiming for ogres. Ogres and normal soldiers got hit. Some fell to the ground and some kept on running. Enemy came close and had collision with the shields. Shields absorbed the collision.

Shielded soldiers were supported by the soldiers behind them. Soldiers quickly started stabbing enemies from sides of the shields. Blood was spilling everywhere. Some enemies were able to kill the shielded soldiers. and ran in the formations but were welcomed by more swords. Fallen shields were quickly grabbed my more soldiers and they made the wall again. Ogres came close too. One ogre grabbed a shield and picked the soldier with it too.

Soldiers quickly ran to his help. They started stabbing the ogre. Ogre roared and threw the shield away. He swung his cleaver and cut down two soldiers from the waist. One soldier jumped on his chest and stabbed his heart. Ogre fell down. Soldier kept on stabbing. Enemies were slowly getting cut down. They killed some soldiers too but clearly were not ready to fight the formations. Fight continued but after some bloodshed, second wave was over. Running back, many enemies were hit by arrows. Lord Clive yelled

"Get ready men, Final wave is coming"

They waited and waited but enemy was not marching their way. Lord Clive turned to see that sun was going down. He went to Lord Artis and talked. They saw enemy going back. Soldiers started putting their swords back in the sheathes. Today was over. Lord Clive ordered the army to come back. Lord Artis yelled

"Today we won Soldiers, be happy"

Sun went down, fires started to rise at different places in the camp. Soldiers were happy to see their friends alive and some were sad because they lost their today. They did not take much damage but they had the taste of enemy power. Lords and commanders gathered into the main tent. They had to make strategy for tomorrow.

Philip: They did not use fireballs today, they could do some serious damage.

Artis: I do not think that they reached here yet.

Clive: We got lucky but tomorrow they will throw their whole army at us.

Salvador: My lord, We can give some archers long bows and horses. If all out fight break out tomorrow then they can ride close to the enemy and target them.

Artis: We need more horses for that.

Salvador: My lord, I can fight on foot.

All lords looked at each other. They all had horses too.

Clive: Well take my horse and my guard's too. We can fight on foot too.

Riendo: Elves did pretty good today but if they bring more Rhinos tomorrow.

Artis: We can break the formation. Rhinos can not turn that quickly. Hit them in the legs.

Theia was also present but her mind was worried about Red. She was waiting for the time which Red told her. Kerk said something and Poif translated.

Kerk: What happened to targeting the officers?

Artis: It can not be done until we can get close. They are sending waves so no officers are present in the front line.

Kerk: One of the rhinos had an officer on it. The one we saw at the negotiations. He killed two of my elves then I lost sight.

Clive: Red shadow?

Kerk: I do not know, he said nothing in the negotiations.

Philip: That is Red shadow. Let's hope he died.

Over at Brett' camp, Brett, Atlan and Adlard were sitting in the main tent. Bryte was standing and Red was nowhere to be found. Brett and Adlard were drinking wine.

Brett: You wanted to test the army, we lost horribly.

Adlard: Do not worry, I sent the weakest soldiers today.

Brett: They can not fight the shielded wall. Tell your soldiers to try to jump over them.

Adlard: Noted, but today they felt that we are weak. Tomorrow they will have surprise. I did not throw fireballs at them. They will give us a benefit too.

Brett: Where is Red?

Bryte: He went in the second wave to test his Boggart. Elves took it down. He made it back alive and killed two elves in the process.

Brett: Now?

Bryte: I do not know, frankly I am scared of him too. I do not want to ask him questions.

Brett: He gave you a honey bunny.

Bryte: I was surprised but she is amazing. Red should feel sorry.

Adlard: Warrior women are best to keep. Hard to handle but if they accept you, you are in heaven.

Brett and Bryte laughed.

Adlard: Brett, if you want one, I can send you from my personal warriors. I have quite a few gems.

Brett: I am honored but I do not want to be distracted right now but I heard about the beauty of Bryte's girl. Definitely want her.

Bryte: Come on Brett.

Brett: What? friends share.

Bryte: Not the wives.

Brett: Ohhhh, she is your wife now.

Bryte: Not yet, but I am planning to do it.

Brett: Not done it yet. Plus After this war is over. You are allowed to take one valley in this land and you can live with her in peace.

Bryte: Not after I know that another man touched her too. You now, last night I knew that she is untouched. That's when I knew that I want her.

Brett: How is that possible, If her beauty is as they say.

Atlan: She is a good fighter and a fierce woman. She would not let Bryte touch her too if King did not ordered it.

Brett: Oh boy, now I want her too. Bryte tomorrow night. Bring her to me.

Bryte: Come on Brett.

Brett: That is an order from your lord Bryte.

Brett's voice got a little hard. Bryte knew he was serious.

Bryte: Brett, can I go to my tent? She instructed me to come quick.

Brett: How do you know? you can not speak their language.

Bryte: we are working on the communication. And she did some hand gestures which showed that she will kill me if I am late.

Brett started laughing. Adlard just smiled and said.

Adlard: Go Bryte, you will be in pain if you upset her.

Bryte smiled and walked back to his tent. His girl said nothing to him but he wanted to be alone with his thoughts. He was tired of standing around and listening to battle plans all day. He came to his tent and entered. Girl was sleeping. Bryte removed his armor and clanking of metal woke her up. She turned and saw Bryte. She just gave him a sleepy smile and

Bryte forgot all his tiredness and tensions. Bryte sat down with her. She sat up. Bryte asked in gestures

"How are you?"

She answered with a smile and her hand over heart.

Bryte heard Atlan talking to someone outside his tent. He asked him if he can translate for some time. Atlan was a busy person. He said that a troll can do this but he will write what they say. Trolls do not speak much. Less is better than none. Bryte asked for the troll and came in. After sometime, same troll which treated Red came in the tent. Bryte gave him a paper and the ink pot. Girl was confused but Bryte said to the troll.

"Ask her, how is she?"

Troll wrote it down and showed her. She replied and troll did the same thing with Bryte.

"I am fine, how about you?"

"I am fine too, I just wanted to know you better"

"Why?"

"Because I have your responsibility now"

"I am in your service"

"You are so beautiful"

"Thank you"

"You are a born fighter?"

"They say, I was born and put to training as soon as I could walk"

"You did not wanted to be a fighter?"

"I always fought, rest is good but I am not allowed to be rested"

"Rest? what do you mean rest?"

"Sitting at home, Like my mother did. She did house work."

"Servant?"

"No, her own house. Looking after her family"

"I can provide you a home if you want"

"My mother said that I am so beautiful that I can marry a King and live in a castle"

"Bad luck for you, you are stuck with a body guard"

She laughed.

"I am not sad, Girls who are in King Adlard's service are in bad condition"

"You are not in my service, I will marry you as soon as this war is over"

Girl's eyes spread a bit.

"Why do you want to marry me?"

"Because I like you"

"But I am already in your service"

"You are ordered to, I do not want to force anything on you"

"Thank you for this, You treat me well"

"I will treat you more good but you will not be allowed to work at our house too"

"Then?"

"I will get you servants and you can rest all day"

"But I heard that only Lords are allowed to keep servants in your world"

"No, Any man who can afford to pay them can have servants"

"Are you able to pay them?"

"Yes, I am friends with Lord Brett. He never asked me about money I spent"

A soldier asked for Bryte from outside the tent. Bryte came out and Soldier said

"Lord Brett instructed your servant to not to come to war tomorrow"

"I do not have a servant"

"The girl"

Soldier turned around and Bryte punched the pole holding the tent. He told Brett that he wanted to make her his wife but he had no choice. Brett was giving him a bright future as his father was in army and his grandfather too. This was his chance to break that line and be a rich man.

Bryte came in, he said to the troll.

"Write, Lord Brett wants you to not to come to fight tomorrow"

Troll wrote it and Girl nodded.

At midnight, Theia started riding towards the grove. Her horse was running full speed. She was worried about Red. After reaching the grove, She tied the horse to a tree and entered. Red was sitting near the pond. Theia took a deep breath and her worries went away with it. Theia came near him and hugged him from the back. Red lifted his hand and slowly pet her face. He said

"I am all right Theia, do not worry"

She sat beside him. He was sewing a wound in his arm. She said

"I was worried, I heard you were taken down by elves"

"Yes, I was testing my new boggart and the damn elves killed it"

"This wound?"

"A horse rider gave it to me, Ludik was a surprise to us"

"Get a proper medic to look at it"

"Too many spies, they would be targeting the officers because of less numbers. A medic can easily poison me, are you fine?"

"I am fine Red, but you are not"

"It is nothing, I have cleared it and now I am just sewing it"

"With needle right? it is called a needle"

"Yes" Red smiled.

"You taught me that"

"I did, I did"

Theia felt relieved. Red was alive and was not injured. She said again

"Shame about the Boggart"

"Yes, he was a good animal"

"When we win, and you will be a prisoner then I will get you a new one"

They both laughed. Theia said again

"Can I sew?"

"Wound?"

"Yes"

"Here, do not go in my arm, just hold the skin together and put the needle in and around"

Red gave her the arm and she started sewing. Blood was spilling a little. Red cleared it with a cloth.

"i can not stay longer Red, They will suspect me"

"I know, you can leave right now but remember if you get hurt or lose the war. Come here on the exact moment. I will come to get you"

"Same goes for you"

She smiled. Red stood up and wrapped his arm in a bandage. They came to Theia's horse and she got up.

She turned the horse and said

"You missed the chance again"

Red smiled and said

"I remembered, but I want it to be happy not tense"

Theia started riding back with heavy heart. She wanted to look back but she was getting the same feeling she had when she showed Red the way to deep forest. It was like she will not see him again. She would not leave the battle ground at any cost and she knew that Red would do the same. They both were ready to die for their sides. She kicked the horse and horse started running faster. She reached the camp and entered. Suddenly Ludik held her horses reins. He said

"Why are you on a horse?"

She was caught. She said

"I was practicing my riding"

"Come on Theia, we need all the horses"

"But I did not volunteer to give my horse"

"Oh, sorry then"

Ludik left the reins. Theia laughed and called him back.

"I was joking Ludik, take the horse"

Ludik smiled and put a sack on horse's mouth. He tied it hard. Theia asked

"What are you doing?"

"New orders, you were not in the meeting"

Ludik took the horse and left. While going back to the tent Theia noticed that Ludik and his men were taking all the horses. She walked in and laid on her bed. Lords had another meeting after she left to meet Red and gave some new orders. She fell asleep while thinking about it.

23

CHAPTER 23

In the morning, When sun rose. Forces were in formations. Enemy was in front and this time, Brett's soldiers were in front. Lords were on foot among the soldiers. They were walking and giving speeches to boost up the morale. Brett was doing the same thing to his soldiers. Both sides were ready to fight.

Lord Clive came in front, everyone went silent. Lord Clive took out his sword and all the soldiers did the same. Lord Clive started to run towards enemy all of a sudden. Whole army did the same thing. Brett did not understand. This was not a wave. They were coming all. Formations were broke. Brett yelled

"Get ready, they are bringing the fight to us"

Shields were brought in front. Lord Clive's army had archers. They were stopping every few steps and firing two arrows at the same time. Brett's soldier's were getting hit because of their numbers. Brett understood that they were not giving them space and avoiding fireballs. It was a good strategy. Bryte took Brett to a high place. Adlard and Atlan were standing there so they could see the battle and give commands. Brett ordered to fire arrows at will.

Archers started firing arrows and took down many of the running soldiers. Lord Clive was the first one to collide with a shield. He hit it with his shoulder, grabbed it with his hand and pulled it with great force. Shielded enemy came forward and Soldiers started getting in the wall. Lord Clive had Lord Philip's fighters with him. They entered and quickly started cutting down enemies. Adlard said

"They broke our wall with one hit"

Lord Clive stabbed the shielded soldier and entered enemy army. Enemies were attacking but he was blocking every attack. Many more shields fell. Lord Artis was attacking on the right side and Lord Philip was attacking on the left side. They left their center a little weak so the enemy was trying to attack the center and the sides were not getting much attention. Lord Artis was finally able to break the wall and Soldiers entered from the right too.

Both armies were losing men quickly. Lord Philip's fighters were cutting necks. They seemed like on a whole another level of skill. Philip entered form the left too. Now it was a all out war. Enemy soldiers were blocked by their own soldiers. They could not attack all together but slowly they were getting in the fight. Brett said

"If they keep this up, they will lose"

Lord Philip was pushing from the left. He was facing difficulties because ogres were present in that direction. He lost many men to ogres. He could not afford that. His soldiers were trying their best to avoid the swords and cleavers of the ogres. Theia was with Lord Clive, She was fighting side by side Lord Clive. Kerk and Poif were fighting with Lord Artis. Whole place was filled with the voices of metal clanking, yelling and painful voices of soldiers. Many were on the ground wounded or dead. Many were trying to fight with wounds. Brett said

"Bring out the boggarts, we will crush them"

Adlard said

"We can not, our soldiers are in front and they will crush them too. Boggarts and fireballs are behind the foot soldiers"

Brett ordered the army to retreat a bit so he can at least bring out the boggarts. His army retreated a bit. Some space was cleared and now both armies were standing face to face. Archers were hitting Brett's soldiers while they were trying to clear way for the boggarts. Some were still fighting and could not retreat in time. Lord Artis was fighting with one of the officers. Lord Artis swung his sword and the enemy blocked it.

He pushed Lord Artis back. Lord Artis came back a few steps and Kerk jumped in. He did not give any chance to the enemy officer. Officer was looking at Artis, Kerk's sword separated his head from the body. Lord Artis was exhausted. He held his sword up again and began walking towards the enemy. Sun was high and soldiers were sweating. Their breath was fast.

They were tired. But they followed the lead of Lord Artis and started to move towards enemy. Lord Clive did the same and Lord Philip too. Lord Clive look down to avoid stepping on a body and saw that it was of General Salvador. He said

"So long, General"

He again started to walk. Enemy had cleared the way for boggarts. Boggarts were making their way to front. With them comes the ogres and trolls. Trolls were new to the soldiers. Lord Artis yelled

"We killed the ogres and the rhinos, do not be afraid men"

Soldiers chanted. Lord Artis could see Brett standing on high ground. He signaled an archer. Archer was not a long bow. His arrows could not reach. He ran and disappeared in the soldiers to find a long bow archer.

Enemy was formed up. Boggarts and ogres came in front. They were ready to charge. Lord Philip came in front of his men. He said loudly

"Soldiers, we have pushed an army back which is bigger than us. All of you and all who have fallen have earned my respect. Now earn back the lands and families these foreigners are trying to snatch away from us"

Soldiers started beating their swords with their armors. Lord Philip turned and yelled

"Come with me and lets send them to hell"

Soldiers yelled and Started running towards the enemy. Lord Artis was already walking but after Philip, he started running too. Lord Clive did the same thing. Adlard said

"They have a death wish"

Brett said nothing. Army was running close to the enemy. Enemy soldiers held their swords tightly. They were ready to welcome them. All the lords knew that they are too deep and now there will be no retreat. They ran with their soldiers following them in to the jaws of death. Earth was trembling with the stepping of running feet. Soldiers were yelling. Their blood and sweat brought them this far. Arrows were flying and finding their way to enemy bodies. Suddenly, from behind the enemy, noise started to rise.

Painful yelling and metal clanking could be heard. Enemy lines got broken. Their soldiers were running from behind and pushing the front soldiers. Trying to get away from something. Front soldiers got disturbed. Their focus got distracted and they got confused where to look. Brett quickly turned and saw horse squads. Ludik was here. Ludik came from behind the enemy. His horse squads were spread and were crushing enemy heads beneath their horses hooves. Some had ropes with sharp blades attached to them. They were cutting enemy soldiers. Rest were facing the horse men swords. Long bows and short bows were also doing their part. Brett yelled

"Ambush, Ambush, enemy is behind you"

As soon as he yelled it. Lords collide with the front soldiers who were distracted. Brett's forces were getting cut from both sides. Lords did not stop. This was their chance. They got their soldiers deep in enemy lines. Enemy soldiers did not know what to do. They started attacking the nearest soldiers. Throats started getting cut. Flesh started dropping from the bodies. Blood was spilling everywhere. Ludik horses were running here and there.

They were the real problem for enemy. They were not stopping for anything. Hit or miss. They did not care. Adlard was yelling orders in his own language. Brett was yelling orders in his own. Both knew that this could be a problem. Lords got to the point where fireball structures were placed. They ordered the soldiers to burn everything. Soldiers took the torches and oil for fireballs and started burning tents, fireball structures and enemies too.

Ogres, trolls and boggarts were their first priority. Ogres and boggarts on fire were running everywhere. Boggarts were in pain and were crushing everything in their way. Enemy army started to separate. They started to run anywhere possible. Adlard saw a large part of their army holding their ground and fighting properly. Adlard asked

"Who is commanding there?"

"Red, it is Red Shadow"

Brett yelled happily. Red was the commander of that part and he was still holding his soldiers together. Brett yelled

"Go to Red, Go to Red"

Ludik saw the enemy scattering and regrouping in small parts. They used their surprise element. He yelled

"Look for the officers and commanders, kill them quick and they will lose"

He started riding alongside a boggart and fighting with his rider. Rider had slightly different cloths then soldiers indicating that he is an officer. One of the soldier threw oil barrel on the boggart. Barrel exploded and Boggart got covered in oil. One of Ludik's horsemen threw a torch and Boggart caught on fire. Boggart started running crazy and the rider jumped to escape the fire. Ludik stopped and before the rider could stand. Ludik stabbed him in his head. Ludik removed his sword from enemy's head. In front of him, he saw Red. Red was fighting alongside his soldiers. Ludik saw that this part of enemy army was stable. Red's sword was dripping with blood showing that he killed a lot of men. Red saw Ludik and his men. He spread his arms with a deadly smile and said

"Hello boys, I am Red shadow. Here to spread Joy and Fun"

Soldiers did not want to fight Red. His bloody armor and sword showed that how skilled warrior is he. He was the sign of terror for everyone. He did not seem to be wounded. Two elves ran towards him. Red picked up a shield and ran towards them too. His guards were left behind. Red jumped up when reached them and struck one with the shield and one with his sword. Sword hit first elf on his face and his whole lower jaw fell on the ground followed by his unconscious body. Other elf was already stunned by powerful knock of the shield. Red rotated his body and swung the sword in the same motion. Sword cut half of the elf's neck. Red pulled the sword out.

Ludik knew that this was bad. He was instructed not to stop but Red could not be killed by a normal soldier.

"Come on Ludik, don't you want to fight me?"

Ludik knew he was trying to make him angry. Red gave him a bloody smile. Ludik saw Lord Philip and his men approaching from the right. He signaled his horse squads and they started swarming the enemy. Lord Philip reached with his men and he started to fight here too. Red started fighting with the sword and shield. He was going for Ludik but he was riding and there were a lot of enemy soldiers in between.

"Red, Red"

Someone yelled and Red turned around. Rio was standing with his sword too. He came close and said

"Theia is badly injured, she told me to tell you that she is going to some spot you instructed her to. But she could not go unseen. I saw a group of Brett's rider going after her"

Red forgot about the fight. He looked around and saw a horse. He ran to it. He jumped and hit the rider on the neck with his shield. Rider fell down. Red got on the horse and started riding. He did not care who he was colliding with. His men or the enemy men. He just wanted to reach Theia quick. Brett saw Red leaving the battle field. He yelled

"Red, where are you going? Red"

He felt a shooting pain in his back and a sword came out his abdomen. His mouth got full of blood and he spat it out. He fell to the ground. He turned around and saw Bryte swinging his sword at Adlard's neck. Adlard was not looking and his head flew in the air. Brett could not believe what happened. His dying eyes just saw Bryte holding his sword towards Atlan who just turned around. Atlan turned around because Adlard's head fell and rolled in front of him. He turned around and said

"Bryte, What are you doing?"

"Killing you I guess"

Atlan saw Ludik and some horsemen coming towards them. He yelled in an inhuman voice and a black smoke covered him. He became a one legged dark shadow. Bryte took two steps back. He did not know what to do. Ludik was shocked too but he did not stop his horse. He slowed his horse and his horsemen came forward. They went straight for the guards who were appointed to protect Brett and Adlard. Ludik rode through them. Bryte was fighting with Atlan. He struck him couple of times but Atlan lifted his hand every time and a black smoke appeared which stopped Bryte's attack.

Ludik came and leaned to attack Atlan. Atlan used his smoke cloud and Ludik felt that he struck a mountain. He lost his balance but jumped off the horse. rolled over and stood up. He came near Bryte. Now Atlan's back was towards battle field and they both were on his left and right. Atlan made a sword out of the smoke. He struck Ludik, Ludik blocked it but felt like a mountain was pushing against him. Atlan made another sword for his other hand. Now he was striking both men. They were blocking and dodging but could not stand on their feet.

Every time Atlan stroke, they felt a tremendous strength behind it. Atlan struck again, Bryte blocked it over his head but could not stand on his feet. Atlan took him to the ground on his knees. A quick whistle spread in the air and an arrow hit Atlan in the back. He turned around and down on the battle field saw Lord Artis with a long bow, he was standing with some archers. Lord Artis fired again, and his long bow archers followed him.

Atlan was hit by four arrows. two in his shadow face and two in his chest. Atlan just roared in inhuman voice. Ludik quickly beheaded Atlan. Atlan's headless body fell to the ground. Dark smoke slowly started disappearing. It disappeared completely and then blood started gushing out of his neck like it was held back by something. Ludik cut Brett's head off and gave all three heads to his horsemen.

"Take them through the war, announce it"

Horsemen took the heads and rode to the battlefield. Ludik got on his horse and went back to the battle field. Bryte just sat on the ground. He killed his friend by his own hands. He left his sword and laid on his back. Enemy saw the heads of their leaders. They started to scatter like roaches. Some chose to fight but Ludik men were killing commanders by targeted hits. This war was about to be over.

Red was riding fast. He had shield in one hand and with one hand he held the reins. He saw no horse in front of him.

"Am I too late?"

Only the heavy breath of the horse and hooves hitting the ground could be heard. Red reached the grove and jumped off the horse. He saw no horses there.

"Shit, I am too late...no, no, no"

He ran in the grove and saw someone sitting at the pond. Body told that it was a girl and she was wearing the armor of Lord Philip. Red quickly walked towards her. He said

"Thank God, you are here. I thought I was too late"

An arrow came from a tree top, Red quickly moved and dodged it. Red got into his fighting stance. He held his shield in front of him. Some elves and men came out from behind the trees. Red got his sword out. Woman at the pond stood up and turned. It was an elf woman but not Theia. Red ran his eyes on the tree tops and saw three archers. He said softly

"Where are you Theia?"

Five Soldiers came running towards him. Red started fighting. He dodged swords and swung his. He got cut on his cheek but managed to kill them. Red was exhausted after the battle and the horse ride. These men were fresh. Red threw his knife and an archer fell down from the tree top.

"Two remain" he thought to himself.

In front of him, three elves and seven soldiers were remaining. They came together. Red rotated his body in circle and then rotated his arm with a delay. He cut one elf and a soldier. An arrow hit in his thigh. Red did not stop and blocked elf's attack on his shield and quickly pierced him in the skull. Another arrow came but missed. Red took out dying elf's throwing knife and threw it on the archer. Archer fell down. Red took his fighting stance again. Soldiers were careful now. He was not as exhausted as they thought he would be.

24

***

EPILOGUE

At the battle field, Theia was standing with lords. Lords were gathered up and their army was looking for the wounded. Enemy wounded were getting killed immediately. Friendlies were taken to the medics. Enemy forces ran away or were captured. Some were hiding and soldiers were finding them in the tents. Heads of the officers and Commanders were lying in front of the lords. Lord Artis kicked some heads around and saw Brett's head. He picked it up and said

"I raised you better than this Brett"

He dropped the head, He started crying. Lord Philip hugged him. Lord Artis said

"He was my son, my only son Philip"

He started crying like a kid. A soldier came and said

"There is no report from the grove my lord"

The word 'grove' got Theia's attention. Lord Clive said

"Send someone"

Everybody started walking. Theia asked Rio

"What about the grove?"

"Where you went to meet Red Theia"

"Who told you?"

"I followed you last night"

Theia was so worried that she did not took proper precautions.

"Which report is coming Rio?"

"We set a trap for Red there"

Theia stopped and grabbed Rio's arm.

"What do you mean?"

"Theia, he was our enemy. I heard you both talking at the grove and in the battle I told him that you are hurt and went to the grove. Brett's riders are behind you and Red left. After he left. Army was commander less and fell quick"

Theia understood the situation. She quickly looked for a horse but Rio grabbed her arm.

"Theia it is done, do not go"

"You betrayed your own brother Rio?" she yelled.

"He was an enemy"

Theia started crying. Lords were gone. Kerk and poif were standing with them.

A soldier came to Kerk, he said

"A horse is coming from the trap. Lord have requested you to join"

Theia quickly got up and ran towards the front where they started the battle. Kerk, poif and Rio ran too.

Lords were standing at the front and were waiting for the rider to come close. Horse came close and they saw Red falling from it. He was alone. He stood with the support of his shield. He had his sword in his hand. one arrow was in his thigh and one was in his abdomen on the left side. He had two big cuts on his body and seemed like he was bleeding too much. Lord Artis yelled

"He is alive, kill him"

Ludik was standing with him. He took out his sword and came forward. He yelled

"You wanted me Red, here I am"

Red paid him no attention. He was barely standing. His eyes were looking here and there. Up and down. He said slowly

"Where are you Theia?"

Ludik came close and yelled

"You wanted me huh?"

Ludik hit him, Red blocked it with his shield. Ludik swung and Red blocked it with his sword. He said again

"Where are you Theia?"

Ludik swung his sword from down to up. Red stepped to the side and struck Ludik with his shield. Ludik nose started to bleed. Red said

"Got you"

Ludik got angry and he did another attack but Red rotated his body in circle and from behind he stabbed Ludik in his back. Ludik fell down. Red fell down too. He lost too much blood. Wind howled. Everybody was silent. Red heard a faint voice

"Let me through"

It was Theia's voice. Red placed his hand on swords handle. With its support, he stood up. Red's eyes were still looking for her. One more arrow hit him in the chest. Red gasped.

"Where are you Theia?"

Sweat and blood was getting in his eyes. He quickly took support of his sword. Everything was becoming slow. He saw Lord Artis ordering archers. Archers released the arrows. They whistled through the air and flew towards Red. Red took his shield in front but could not do it in time. His left side got three arrows in it. His legs got hit with some arrows too. He stood up for a second. His hands were shaking.

"Where are you Theia?"

His hand could not hold his shield anymore. He dropped the shield. A soldier started running towards him. From behind him, he saw Theia came in front running. Red saw her face which had some dirt on it. Her blue eyes were full of tears. Her hair were pitch black. She started running towards him. Just one soldier in between. One last hurdle. As soon as soldier came close. Red collected his remaining strength and picked his sword up pointing at the soldier. Soldier was running and could not stop in time. Sword went in his chest. Red pushed the sword with all his strength and it came out the back. Red fell on his knees. Theia got closed to him and held him in her arms. She laid his head on her lap. She was crying. Red said

"I was looking....... all over for you my love"

"You found me Red, You found me"

Red lifted his hand slowly. He removed the dirt on her face.

"your face ...got....dirty"

Theia just kept on crying. Dirt from her face dropped in Red's eye. Theia quickly started rubbing his eyes to clear blood and dirt. Red's hand fell down. He smiled at Theia for the last time. Theia put her hand on his cheek and smiled back with tears. She kept on crying. Red was dead. Everybody was silent. They did not know what was happening except the Lords and Rio. Theia kept on crying.

Everybody was happy in the Land of Draound. Battle was over. Army was hunting any enemy soldiers who ran. Lords were throwing feasts and people were feeling alive. Fallen comrades were being remembered. Their lives were getting celebrated. Bryte was given the valley of Henry because of his last minute deal with Lord Artis. A spy saw him reacting after Brett's orders regarding his girl. He informed Lord Artis and this deal was made. Bryte was now a lord with his girl. He was happy in his new castle. Rio left with Lord Philip. Ludik was no more so he was the new Ludik for Lord Philip. Lord Artis returned to his valley and took back the charge.

Elves were walking in the Blue Forest. Blue forest was as beautiful as it always was. A passage door was opened in the forest and it was time for the elves to back. Theia was walking with poif. Behind her, two elves were holding a stretcher. It had Red's body on it. Theia asked lords to take Red's body. They had no objection. They came to the passage. Elves started walking in and disappearing in the dark. Before Theia could enter Poif grabbed her hand

"Are you sure Theia? you lived your whole life here"

"Yes Poif, I want to sleep forever with Red"

"Red cannot be his real name"

"No, I asked his brother and he told me his real name is....."

A loud growl echoed in the Forest. Theia and Poif both looked in that direction but could not see anything. She smiled at Poif and said

"I guess Red does not want you to know his real name"

Poif smiled back and walked in. Theia came to the stretcher and held Red's cold hand. She smiled at him.

Then they all walked in and passage door closed. Leaving the Blue Forest as it was. Calm beautiful and deadly.